A Not
So Rosy
Vintage

Holt Jacobs Mystery - Book 3

Lily Stirling

~ To Sam ~
Thanks for being my older brother.

CONTENTS

CHAPTER 1

"**Y**ou expect me to sleep on the pink unicorn bed?" I tugged at my styled hair.

Juniper giggled. My baby sister had spent her life perfecting the art of pushing my buttons. I should have expected trouble. "Come on, Holt." She practically danced with excitement. "Paul got here first. He chose the bed with the rocket ships."

"How"—I began pacing from the twin bed with a rocket ship comforter to the other bed, which had a pink unicorn comforter—"come Rose's Vineyard is fancy enough to have guest lodgings but doesn't have basic bedding?"

My sister lifted a shoulder like she was clueless, but her lips twitched.

"Juniper," I growled. "Did you request this?"

Her mouth dropped open in shock. Juniper made her living as an airbrushed, supposedly approachable social media personality, and I wasn't buying the act.

Taking a step toward her, I asked, "What did you do?"

Juniper was attempting to back toward the door, but since she was doubled over laughing, she wasn't making much progress. The closer I got to Juniper, the harder she laughed. "Your face..." she managed.

I was about to pounce when my girlfriend, Brittany, appeared in the doorway. She'd taken her black hair out of its ponytail and let it hang around her shoulders. For a moment the sight distracted me from the unicorn monstrosity.

Britt looked from me, to Juniper, to the pink unicorn bedspread. Her lips trembled, but she didn't laugh. "Are you getting settled?" she asked.

It's one thing to wrestle my sister to the floor like we're kids without an audience, but I wasn't prepared to do it with my girlfriend watching.

Instead, I said, "I wanted the rocket ships."

So instead of acting like a child, I sounded like one.

"The whole point of this is to give Paul a nice vacation," Brittany said, a sparkle in her brown eyes.

Paul getting a nice vacation was the excuse Juniper had given, but since it was my sister, I doubted the sincerity. And to be clear, I wasn't at Rose's Vineyard for Paul. The only reason I was here was to keep my sister from telling my girlfriend all the sibling dirt she had on me.

Brittany had just moved to Seattle so we could go on dates that weren't over a webcam. Too much alone time with Juniper and she might run shrieking back to Oregon.

"I'd do anything to make sure Paul has a good time," Juniper said, trying to keep a straight face.

"And special requesting astronaut sheets?"

Juniper popped a hip. "I admit nothing. But Paul loved the rockets. And they didn't have specialty blankets in jail."

Once the words were out of her mouth, we all froze and looked toward the door. Luckily, Britt's twin brother wasn't there, and neither was his short yet intimidating girlfriend.

"I think Paul and Sienna are still walking around the property," Juniper said, her shoulders relaxing.

A few months ago Paul had been in jail for a murder he hadn't committed before I rode in on a white horse to prove his innocence...Okay, so there was no white horse, and Juniper would argue it was mostly good luck. Still, Britt, Paul, and Sienna had all thanked me.

Then—like the trip wasn't weird enough—Chouzie padded into my bedroom.

I frowned at the majestic chow chow. "Juniper, this July you said he was a borrowed dog. Now it's September. When are you supposed to return him?"

"Don't listen to him," Juniper cooed, ruffling the chow chow's reddish mane. "You're never going away."

"Won't the owners want their moneymaker back?" I don't follow my sister or the chow chow on social media, but supposedly Chouzie's a superstar.

Juniper chewed at her lip, "They, uh, kind of can't have him back."

"Wait. Are you a dognapper?"

Tossing back her hair, Juniper played self-righteous. "No, genius. They died in a plane crash. Poor Chouzie's an orphan."

Brittany gasped like a villain had been unmasked on a *Scooby-Doo* episode. When I raised an eyebrow, she shook her head. "Your family is nothing like mine."

"Is that a good thing?"

All Britt did was wink before leaving.

"This is your fault," I whisper-shouted to Juniper.

"My fault? You're the one who introduced me to Brittany," Juniper whisper-shouted back.

"Why would you plan a trip with my girlfriend and her family?"

Juniper put her hands on her hips. "You were in the room when we made the plans. You never said anything."

I pointed a finger in her face. "I was asleep when you made the plans."

"So? I was alone in a room with someone I barely knew. I had to think of something to say."

I glared at her. We both knew Juniper never ran out of things to say.

Brittany reappeared, and her lips quirked at having caught us mid-fight. "I was heading down early for our first wine tasting."

"Can I join you?" I asked, sliding on my blazer so I could fully look the part of a fancy businessman on holiday.

"I was hoping you would," Britt said.

"You coming?" I asked Juniper.

She shook her head. "You go ahead. I need to finish getting Chouzie settled. I'll catch up."

"Okay." I was surprised Juniper wasn't tagging along, but maybe she was planning a grand entrance at the tasting room.

I offered Brittany my arm and escorted her out of the suite. As we walked down the two flights of stairs to get to the ground floor, Brittany asked in a low voice, "Did you ask Juniper?"

"No," I said. "I was about to when she distracted me with the fairy princess bed."

Britt's eyes sparkled, but she didn't comment on the bedding and instead returned to the question that was bugging her. "I'd like to know if she's paying for the trip. I'm happy to chip in."

"Yeah," I said, but I didn't super care about giving Juniper money. I was definitely suspicious of the all-expenses-paid vacation Juniper claimed had been offered to her and her guests, but if it was a lie and Juniper was paying for part of it, that was a decision Juniper had come to all on her own.

Still, it was strange.

Either Rose's Vineyard was willing to feed and board five people for three nights as a trade for exposure on my sister's social media, or Juniper wanted this trip bad enough to lie and pay out of pocket.

Supposedly my sister made good money as an influencer. Still, I'd like to think my job as a full-time engineer paid better.

"You'll tell her about the money?" Brittany asked.

"Uhh...doubtful." I stopped walking as we got to the landing. Britt was opening her mouth to argue, but I held up my hand. "I know my sister. If I offered her a blank check, she'd take it without asking why."

"Maybe." Britt's face was beginning to turn emotionless as she considered the problem. "But you think it's weird?"

"Absolutely," I said. "But it's Juniper. She easily could have been offered this trip and not checked what strings were attached."

Brittany nodded, but her face remained impassive. "I'd like to know what's going on."

I winked. "Come on, you're acting like me right before one of my sisters tells me to lighten up and have some fun."

"Aren't you worried?"

It was a serious question, and in an instant all my playfulness evaporated. "Not worried. But suspicious." I caught Britt's eyes. "We'll figure this out."

Before Britt could reply, her phone began ringing. "It's Sienna," she said and then answered. "Hello?"

I moved farther into the lobby to give Britt some privacy. The whole compound for Rose's Vineyard was trying to be the height of sophistication, which is how the building we were sleeping in had earned the pretentious name of Rose's Repose.

It was an odd building, too big to be a house but too small to be a hotel. It was a newer construction, masquerading as something grand from a previous century. Stained glass windows were sprinkled through the rooms, reflecting a rainbow of colors. We were staying in one of the two big suites on the third floor, complete with two bathrooms, a living room, and a kitchenette. The second floor had an assortment of single rooms with attached restrooms.

Aside from the check-in desk, the lobby was a large room split into two sitting areas with a large fireplace in the middle. Otherwise, there was a dining area and what I can only assume was an industrial kitchen past a swinging door.

The decor in the lobby was a tacky amount of pictures of smiling friends through the decades. The woman who was in the center of most of the photos was very striking. It wasn't just her face, or hair, or the glasses with frames that never seemed to change, but the way she carried herself that had me looking closer.

"Holt?" Britt asked.

I didn't look away from the images as I said, "Yeah?"

"Paul and Sienna will meet us on the path to the tasting room."

Brittany would have gone straight outside, but I was stalled by the photos of the friend group. I don't know why. While the woman with the glasses had caught my attention, I rarely look at pictures of people I know and definitely don't have the time to judge the photo-worthy moments of strangers.

Still, there was something about the images. Every picture showed the same group of two men and three women, almost always with the woman in glasses posed in the middle.

"Ready?" Britt asked, choosing not to question my interest in the strangers.

"Ready," I said and turned away from the photos to focus on my girlfriend.

Brittany and I headed outside to the path between the house and Rose's Tasting Room. It was one of those surprisingly hot September days that had me sweating in my button-up and blazer. Meanwhile, Brittany looked comfortable in a sleeveless summer dress.

Aside from the extra sweat, I was feeling good about my appearance. My wavy dark blond hair was expertly styled, and my suit was the perfect dressy yet casual look for a winery and was expertly tailored for my six-one frame.

Then I saw Paul.

You know how Brittany is the most attractive woman in the world, with her black hair falling to her shoulders, beautiful brown eyes, and the confidence that comes from daily saving lives as a paramedic? Well, imagine what her professional fisherman twin brother looked like.

The one time I'd met him had been near the end of his time in jail, when he'd begun letting himself go. At the time I hadn't considered him handsome—though it's understandably hard to pull off a jumpsuit.

But the Paul who was smiling and holding hands with his girlfriend, Sienna, was a completely different person. Gone was the scraggly beard, replaced by a sharp jaw. His hair was cut, and he wore a linen button-up shirt with the top two buttons undone. Plus he had the natural swagger that came from working outside.

Reason number thirty-seven why this trip was a bad idea: Someone here was hotter than me.

I tried to hide my jealousy as hugs and handshakes went around. Sienna went on tippy-toes, and I bent down to let her kiss my cheek. A little odd. But Sienna rocked the whole really short, dreadlocks, fair-trade clothes, and organic deodorant thing. Somehow she could pull off kissing men's cheeks.

Paul wasn't jealous seeing his girlfriend kiss my cheek, and Britt wasn't jealous watching Sienna kiss her boyfriend. So I was still the only one jealous—and it was because I hadn't mentally prepared for how handsome Paul was. It's petty, but I didn't appreciate being demoted from the leading man to the best friend.

"So good to see you." Paul clapped my back.

"Uh-huh," I said, not quite up to returning the compliment. Plus, saying *I wish you were uglier* would be rude.

As we started walking to the building with a fancy sign proclaiming Rose's Tasting Room, Sienna moved to walk beside me.

"Holt, we go way back, right?" she asked.

I wouldn't call meeting two months ago as *way back*, but I nodded.

"Then tell me, did Juniper really get an all-expenses paid trip as a trade since she's posting about the winery on social media?"

I shrugged. "If my sister's to be believed..."

"Don't imply Juniper's a pathological liar," Brittany said—like she hadn't just been talking about how unbelievable Juniper's story was.

"Right. My sister would never lie," I said, not really caring if Sienna caught the sarcasm.

Brittany, being more diplomatic, said, "We don't have anything to disprove Juniper's story of an all-expenses-paid vacation for her and guests."

"If it's true, the winery must be desperate," Paul said.

"That's what I thought," I agreed.

We had to stop our speculation about the winery's financials since we'd arrived at the tasting room. The theory they were desperate enough to invite an influencer did hold weight, because the parking lot was empty of cars. There were absolutely no customers.

I did some quick mental math. Rose's Vineyard had been in business for around thirty years. It was early afternoon on a Thursday. Not exactly a time to be packed, but you'd expect there'd be a book club or an office party getting tipsy in the corner. Could they really be relying on Juniper's social media to drum up business?

And what would she take pictures of? While the main floor of Rose's Repose could have old-world charm if they threw away all the framed photos, the tasting room had no character. I mean, it looked like a tasting room. There were decorative barrels and fake grapes, with plenty of goblets. But there was no spark—nothing to tie it all together.

Britt's hand tightened around my arm. "Don't you love it?"

My mouth twitched. Was Britt being serious? I couldn't tell. I was about to ask, when we were greeted by two men and two women.

A well-put-together woman in her late fifties stepped forward. "Are you Juniper's party?"

"We are," Britt said.

The woman gave a professional smile—the way her face *didn't* wrinkle, I suspected she'd gotten Botox. "Wonderful. I'm Hannah, and this is my husband, Brad."

The man standing beside her was equally well dressed. He gave a sleazy smile that hinted he'd been (or still was) a ladies' man.

"I'm Sue," the other woman said. She had her short hair in tiny pigtails and was wearing a pastel dress she'd probably sewn from a pattern.

"Joe," was all the other man said. He was dressed in dark work pants and a black T-shirt.

While Paul and Sienna were introducing themselves, I whispered to Brittany, "Why do I recognize them?"

"They're from the photos," Britt whispered back.

I frowned, trying to recall the images. The woman I immediately remembered wasn't one of these four. She may not have been conventionally beautiful, but there was something striking about her dark hair and glasses.

Suddenly an image of the five of them on a boat came to mind, and I took a step back. The photo had to be at least twenty years old, but aside from aging, they all looked exactly the same.

I stared at them as everyone around me made small talk.

It was like I was watching a reunion episode of a nineties sitcom.

Before you get too upset, let me just say, I'm as mad about stereo-typing and placing people in boxes as the next guy. But how else are you supposed to remember people?

Hannah with her designer clothes and blond hair was playing the role of Hot Hannah. She'd be effortlessly attractive and extremely competent. Brad, who was watching Sienna instead of his wife, was Bad Brad. His role would be that of *lovable rogue*. Sue, with her pigtails and homemade clothes, was Quirky Sue. If their lives were a TV show, anytime the writers ran out of plots, they'd give her a new talent or hobby. While Joe, with his forgettable face and generic clothes, was none other than Average Joe. The everyman who needed jokes explained to him.

We were missing the star. The woman with the glasses had yet to show up, but there wasn't a doubt in my mind that she was the big-name superstar who held the group together.

Had they actually made a pact thirty years ago as to what cliché each person brought to the table? From what I could tell, there had been little deviations in character from the photos taken thirty years ago. Except now there was graying hair and wrinkles—or in the case of Hot Hannah, dyed hair and Botox.

Average Joe cleared his throat, hands shoved deep in his pockets. "This way to your table."

As we walked, I made sure Bad Brad was in front of me and Britt. It might have been cavemannish, but I didn't want him watching Brittany walk.

An effort had been made at our table. A tablecloth was the base for expertly lain goblets and bottles, plus an impressive array of appetizers.

I'll drink wine, but I'm not a *wine drinker*, and sitting around while a bunch of people pretend to be fancy is exhausting. I'd already worked a half day and driven for a couple of hours to get here. Could I skip the tasting, steal a tray of finger foods, and eat them alone in a corner?

Britt gave my arm a squeeze and shook her head. Was I that easy to read?

My nineties sitcom friends were behaving oddly, each of them looking at the other and none of them talking. If this were a reunion episode of a nineties show, it would be a deleted scene where all the actors forgot their lines.

Was this how they were with all their customers? No wonder business was in a slump.

Then the door opened, and everyone visibly relaxed.

Juniper had arrived.

How was my sister able to do that? And why was I unable to create a similar effect?

Juniper chattered with the hosts, filmed tiny clips, and took photos. The rest of us were completely forgotten as the reunion cast of *Rose's Vineyard* fawned over my sister.

I began eating appetizers. I was sampling my third when Paul joined in. Sure, under normal circumstances it would have been rude to start eating before the guest of honor, but today it didn't matter. We'd become invisible the moment Juniper arrived.

An early sampling of the wine was a different story. It was all still bottled, and even I wasn't going to start uncorking bottles at a free tasting.

At first Juniper enjoyed the attention from our hosts, but as time passed I could tell she was getting irritated. Bad Brad referencing the gold swimsuit she'd worn on vacation three years ago made everyone uncomfortable enough that the praise died down.

Juniper bent toward me from her spot at the head of the table. "Do you have any food recommendations?"

My mouth was full of a specialty cheese on a fancy cracker. For answer, I handed her one, and she nibbled it as our hosts regrouped.

After a few whispers back and forth, Hot Hannah picked up a bottle with a flourish and said, "Let's start with this lovely Cabernet." And just like that, the tasting had commenced.

Bad Brad and Hot Hannah were the presenters, opening different bottles and taking turns giving little asides. Like, Bad Brad picked up a bottle and said, "This Pinot pairs marvelously with this goat cheese we buy from the local farmers market."

As he began removing the cork, Hot Hannah added, "On our thirteenth wedding anniversary, we bought this corkscrew in Venice. The one-of-a-kind handle is Venetian glass made by local artists..."

Both Brad's and Hannah's lines were delivered with a stiffness that showed just how scripted they were, while all Quirky Sue and Average Joe did was stand and watch from behind the bar.

For some reason I kept checking the doors, waiting for the woman in glasses. Once she showed up, the whole charade would go smoother. But bottle after bottle was sampled, yet the woman from the photos never appeared.

I'm already not a huge fan of wine. I'll drink it if it's the only option, but hearing fake nineties stars talk about nutty bouquets really wasn't my jam. The cheese was good, though. If it was sourced from a local farmers market, Britt and I would need to make a pit stop on the way back to Seattle.

The whole affair was so stilted, Juniper had to use every ounce of charm to make it fun. Britt and I held hands, more or less there for the ride, while Sienna kept whispering in Paul's ear, making him laugh. If we really were here for Paul (as Juniper claimed), at least he was having a nice time.

Paul leaned back to whisper in Sienna's ear. Quirky Sue and Hot Hannah tracked the movement. The way they watched him, you'd think he was the lead singer of their favorite boy band.

Since when was Paul super hot? It wasn't fair.

I'm not exactly proud of this, but I unbuttoned the top two buttons on my shirt and wrapped an arm around the back of Britt's chair to better show off my physique.

Britt was too observant. Her eyes went from Paul, to the winery ladies, then to me. When her eyes sparkled, I fought the urge to squirm. Was I being ridiculous?

Brittany and I were in uncharted relationship waters. Beyond the fact we were exclusive and I could officially call her my girlfriend, I still didn't know where we were.

In the span of four months, we'd met, had a joint vacation, and she'd found a new job in Seattle so we could go on real dates. But she'd only finished moving a couple of weeks ago, and we'd barely seen each other before Juniper's trip to Rose's Vineyard.

Before I began dating Brittany, the longest relationship I'd had was a few months in college. And when you're thirty, a few months in college no longer counts.

Brittany, on the other hand, had been engaged to a Coast Guard hunk and would be married right now if he hadn't died.

What were the chances she'd realize I was a huge mistake and move back to Oregon?

"What's wrong?" Brittany whispered, the ghost of a scar visible by her right eyebrow.

Sienna and Paul were sharing an inside joke, while Juniper was filming herself talking about wine. Everyone else was so happy.

I managed a grin. "Nothing."

Britt's analyzing paramedic eyes scanned over me.

Squeezing her hand, I shrugged. "I guess the drive wore me out."

She nodded slowly. Not quite believing me, but the middle of a wine tasting wasn't ideal for follow-up questions.

I let out a breath when Brittany refocused on the wine Hot Hannah was talking about. What was wrong with me? A moment ago my only problem was Paul being hotter than me.

I studied Britt's profile. Would she think I was too neurotic or too clueless when it came to being a boyfriend?

"Holt." Juniper was waving her phone in my face.

"What?"

"Film this."

Usually this would be her husband Jude's job, but he wasn't able to make it. Supposedly, Jude was on a boring business trip. If you ask me, he's probably a spy—he once somersaulted behind a couch. But if he is a spy, both he and my sister haven't admitted it.

I pressed film and had to stifle multiple yawns while Juniper gave an over-the-top toast about friendship and good wine.

At one point, when Juniper was choking herself up about something, Britt squeezed my leg and whispered at me to be nice.

Had my groan been audible?

I had gray hairs by the time Juniper's toast was over and I was allowed to stop recording.

Thankfully, that signaled an end to the affair. All that was left was Quirky Sue announcing there'd be a light dinner at Rose's Repose in an hour. I was pretty stuffed on cheese, but if the supper was anything like the appetizers, I'd need to make room. So far Quirky Sue's cooking was the only highlight.

With the official tasting over, the rest of our party stayed to chat with our hosts. But I needed some air. Would it be too clingy to ask Britt to join me? Would it be rude not to ask? Were my hands sweating? Catching her eye, I tilted my head toward the exit. She shook her head, and I nodded. That was fine. I was out of the tasting room the instant I knew she wasn't coming with me.

Probably for the best. Brittany and I had already spent the drive together before the tasting. If absence makes the heart grow fonder, what damage does too much proximity do? I wouldn't want Britt to get sick of me on the first day.

I started my walk in between rows and rows of grapevines that stretched out in all directions. Far off to my right were sounds of farm equipment in the middle of harvesting. The view wasn't particularly intriguing, so after I'd gone a little ways, I turned around and walked along gravel footpaths around the winery's various outbuildings.

I was by the main entrance to what had to be the actual winery, where they fermented and bottled the grapes, when a woman in a white sweater came stumbling out of the open double doors. Sure, this was a winery, but it wasn't even 4:30 p.m., and from the way she swayed, she'd been sampling quite a lot of product.

She stumbled to face me. I was surprised that the woman's sweater was dyed red with spilled wine. She was around my age with brown hair escaping a clip and tumbling around her face.

She moved toward me, and I fought the urge to back away. She said a word that was hard to understand. It kind of sounded like *Holt*, but this stranger couldn't know my name. Had she said *Help*?

How much help could I be? I managed not to run away but couldn't make myself go to her. I stood stock-still as she stumbled to me.

Half catching her when she reached me, I expected the reek of wine. But she didn't smell like wine. She smelled like...I almost dropped her.

She wasn't covered in wine. She was covered in blood.

Then I saw the top of a corkscrew sticking out of her chest. Why hadn't Brittany come with me? Paramedics know what to do in these situations. Former lifeguards with lapsed first aid certifications don't.

"Brittany!" I yelled.

The woman gave a little cry before going limp in my arms.

"BRITTANY!!!"

Chapter 2

B ritt is phenomenal at her job, but even she can't bring back the
dead. Our light supper was postponed in favor of yellow crime
scene tape and police interviews.

Not only was my casual suit ruined, but it was also considered
evidence. I was photographed on all sides before plastic booties were
put over my shoes and an officer escorted me to our rooms. I was given
evidence bags and instructed to place my clothes inside. Once I handed
over the bags, I'd be allowed to shower.

Brittany received similar treatment, being handed her own set of
evidence bags and being directed to use the suite's other shower.

My shoes, pants, jacket, and button-up were all dutifully bagged. I
stood in the locked bathroom in my socks and underwear. Did they
need those too? I'd forgotten to ask. I didn't see any blood on them,
but what if leaving them out made me more suspicious?

While I've never been in the habit of giving away my underwear,
I made an exception. So I neatly folded my underclothes and added
them to the evidence bags. I passed them through the cracked bathroom door to the waiting officer, then proceeded to shower.

I took a long shower, scrubbing every part of me multiple times.
Halfway through toweling off, I decided I still wasn't clean and
hopped back in for an additional shower.

The police were probably waiting with more questions, but they'd just have to wait.

The image of the woman stumbling toward me suddenly filled my vision, and I tried to block out the memory. My timing had been pretty bad. A little earlier and I could have actually helped her or even stopped the killer. And if I'd shown up two minutes later, she would have already been dead, and I wouldn't be covered in evidence with police low-key wondering if I'd done it. At least I never touched the corkscrew. My fingerprints *not* being on the murder weapon had to be worth something.

When I finally left the bathroom, our rooms were empty. Brittany and the officer who'd taken my clothes were both gone. After dressing in a pair of joggers and a pullover, I went down the two flights of stairs. My party and the fake sitcom actors were grouped in the ground-floor living area. Chairs had been moved to make it all one big space, and at least five police officers were there with plenty more police or techs still at the crime scene.

I froze. Aside from the officers, everyone else was in their wine-tasting clothes. Well, aside from Brittany. But she'd at least put on another summer dress. Why had I dressed like a college student? Paul would look that much hotter—not that it's a competition.

If Juniper hadn't spotted me, I would have snuck up and changed. As it was, I slid onto the couch next to Brittany.

The person who was speaking had to be the detective in charge. Instead of a uniform, he wore a light blue button-up with a tie. Here's the thing, though, the guy looked like a child—or maybe a teen. There's clean-shaven and then there's *no facial hair has ever grown here*.

He was a kid. Was Cop Kid really in charge?

He was saying, "...driver's license, her name is Natasha Ryan. Do any of you know her?"

Our hosts shook their heads along with the rest of us.

Cop Kid nodded, like it was to be expected. "Do any of you recognize her?"

An officer had a zoomed-in picture of the driver's license on a tablet and showed it to each of us. When it came to me, I was surprised by how pretty the woman was—I wished my driver's license pic had turned out so well.

"Holt?" Brittany asked.

How long had I been staring? Clearing my throat, I shook my head. "No, I don't know her."

The image made its way around the group, and when it got to Juniper, she scrunched her nose. She looked from the photo, to me, and back to the photo.

"Do you know her?" the officer asked.

Juniper made direct eye contact with the cop and said, "I've never met her." Her gaze shifted to me a moment later. Why did I feel like I was missing something?

They asked where everyone was after the tasting. Juniper, Britt, and Sienna all had the sense to stay in a group and could alibi one another. Unfortunately, Paul had gone back to our rooms, while I was wandering the grounds.

Our hosts didn't fare much better. Quirky Sue was alone in the kitchen. Average Joe had been fixing a spigot in the vineyard. Hot Hannah had been powdering her nose. And Bad Brad was in his office, working on invoices.

The six of us were all alone and had no alibis.

When the police took Paul to get his full statement, Brittany and Sienna shared a worried look. While I've been suspected of a few crimes in my day, Paul had actually spent months in jail for something he didn't do.

So much for this trip being a relaxing fresh start.

It wouldn't go well if I said *I knew Juniper's winery trip was a bad idea*. But I'd seriously known it and warned them.

Also, supper had been postponed indefinitely. It was all dependent on the police, and they were giving no signs that they would be done with us anytime soon. All the cheese I'd eaten at the tasting had worn off, and I wanted supper.

The sudden image of that woman stumbling toward me popped up. I shivered. Was this really happening again?

Murders are very inconvenient.

The police interviewed us one at a time in an empty guest room on the second floor. I waited my turn on the couch. From time to time I felt Juniper's eyes on me. If she was trying to psychically communicate with me, I couldn't understand a word.

What had she said about Natasha Ryan? *I've never met her.* What had she left unsaid? What was she trying to communicate with her eyes?

Once Sienna was called to give her statement, Juniper took her chair that was next to my spot on the couch. Then Juniper leaned over like she planned on whispering in my ear. Since someone whispering right next to my ear can feel like hundreds of baby spiders crawling down my spine, I scooted closer to Britt so Juniper couldn't reach.

Before my sister could launch a counterstrike, Hot Hannah had crouched in front of Juniper's chair—quite impressive since Hannah was wearing a tight skirt and heels (not that I was looking).

While Hot Hannah spoke quietly, I was able to hear what she said. "I know that woman dying is a tragedy, but I hope it won't affect our arrangement."

"Arrangement?" Juniper repeated.

"Well"—Hot Hannah paused as she found the right way to spin what she wanted—"not only do we hope you continue your stay, but if you remember, in our contract there was a clause that stated you couldn't say anything detrimental about Rose's Vineyard."

"Uh-huh." Heat crept up Juniper's face. When we were kids, that meant she was about to start screaming. But now my sister was an adult with a job to do.

Juniper bit her lip and nodded slightly. "I have no intention of breaching my contract," she said.

"Wonderful," Hot Hannah said with an overpracticed smile. She wobbled as she stood up and walked to where Bad Brad had been watching the whole exchange.

"Did you hear that?!" Juniper kept her voice quiet, but there was no hiding the anger. "What was Hannah thinking? Of course I wouldn't post about the murder. My followers like escapism. Fun adventures. Not true crime."

Wait. Was my sister upset about Hannah questioning her professionalism?

"Also pretty bad to be talking about marketing before the body's even cold," I added.

"Right, and that." But it didn't seem like Juniper had really heard me. Before we could talk more about Hannah's interruption, Juniper was being summoned to give her statement.

When it was my turn, the interview didn't take very long. They'd gotten most of the info they needed from me at the crime scene.

Brittany was the last person from our group to be interviewed. I passed her in the hallway and fought the desire to wrap my arms around her until the world slowed down. But I controlled myself and joined Juniper, Sienna, and Paul where they stood by the lobby exit. Their faces were serious, and they were talking in low tones.

I didn't wait to hear what they were discussing. Instead, I interrupted Juniper with the question of the hour. "Is there a plan for supper?"

Juniper wrinkled her nose, Paul looked confused, and Sienna was—I'm not quite sure what...scandalized...? Incredulous?

Whatever Sienna thought, she was the first to reply. "There isn't a current supper plan."

"Sorry." Juniper patted my back. "Holt has unique ways of dealing with stress," she said, like Paul and Sienna needed an explanation.

"This isn't stress. This is hunger," I said, my voice rising higher than intended.

Paul took a deep breath, and some of the tension he'd been holding melted away. "I could eat."

"Well, under the circumstances, I don't want to ask Sue for a meal," Sienna said.

"Agreed. We don't want to be too crass," Juniper said before I could answer.

"This isn't a hard decision," I said. "If we're not eating here, we're driving to a restaurant."

Juniper had her phone out, and in a few seconds she was recommending a nearby truck-stop diner that had five-star burgers.

Paul loved burgers. He loved them so much, the first thing he did after being released from jail was get a cheeseburger. All he said was, "Sounds good," but it was the stamp of approval we needed.

"I'll drive," I said.

"Shotgun!" Juniper called.

"Nice try." I punched her shoulder. "But Brittany has a permanent right to sit shotgun in my car."

"How permanent?" Juniper asked, latching on to the wrong part of my comment.

"Um...well...you know..." I was still trying to find the right words when I realized everyone's eyes weren't on me but on something behind me.

I knew Britt was there even before Sienna said, "Hi, Brittany."

Britt had definitely heard me. Her eyes were wide, and while she was amused, I couldn't tell if she was pleased. She hadn't lived in Seattle a month and I was throwing out words like *permanent*. On a scale of zero to bad, how much trouble was I in?

Juniper giggled.

I ignored everyone and walked to the car. I was hungry, a woman had died in my arms, and I'd given away my underwear. I was dangerously close to having a meltdown. If Juniper goaded me into a relationship conversation, I'd end up losing my temper and saying something stupid. Question was, would I be trying to break up or propose?

Brittany was the first person to join me in the car, and I was tempted to snap at her for no other reason than I was cranky. But I restrained myself by squeezing the steering wheel. She didn't say anything, and slowly the other three loaded into the back seat. My foul mood was infectious, and it was a quiet drive to the restaurant.

As we walked in, we were greeted with the restaurant's decor of hundreds of license plates from various states and decades. They were plastered on every inch of wall space that wasn't being utilized for a TV or a window. Even the ceiling fans had license plates attached. What were the chances one would fly off and decapitate me?

Once we were seated, Juniper brightened the party with her special charm. Conversation flowed around me, yet I didn't pay attention to what they said—it was like a white noise machine.

So I sat in silence, being that rude guy on his phone while the rest of the table talked. Occasionally I sensed Juniper's curious eyes on me, and every now and again I caught Brittany or Sienna sharing worried glances or watching Paul.

I wished Juniper could be a little more like me. Her high energy was doing an excellent job of hiding just how awful the day was. Is it bad I missed the quiet of the tense drive over?

"Did anyone see her arrive?" I blurted to the table, not waiting for a lull.

Paul set down the french fry that was halfway to his mouth. For a moment there was a twinkle in his eyes that mirrored Britt's. "Is this how he was in Amelia's Haven?"

"Yes," Britt said.

"Worse," Juniper said.

I tried to kick Juniper under the table, but she dodged and I hit Paul. His eyes flicked from me to Juniper before resting on his sister. "Something tells me they got into more fights then we did."

Brittany's eyes twinkled. "It's because they don't share the psychic twins bond."

"Does it count if my mom has a psychic bond with me?" I half grumbled.

Juniper successfully kicked me under the table. "Don't bad talk Mom."

I raised my right hand. "I would never."

Sienna refocused the conversation by asking, "Does anyone know when Natasha got to the winery?"

There was a pause where we all looked at the other people around the table.

"I don't think the police gave us that information," Britt answered when no one spoke up.

"Did anyone see or hear a car?" I asked. "Or maybe she walked past a window?"

"No, Holt," Juniper said. "You're the only one who knew her." Again Juniper's eyes were trying to convey something, but as Brittany had so conveniently pointed out, we don't share a psychic bond.

Britt caught the tension and tried to cover with a half laugh. "Holt's the only one who *saw* her. He doesn't *know* her."

Juniper batted her eyes, all innocence. "My mistake."

Did Juniper think I knew her? Picturing Natasha with the hair falling around her face, I couldn't come up with a clear image. And that driver's license photo...Well, no one looks normal in those. Still, how would Juniper even know if I was friends with that woman? I lived in Seattle, and Juniper lived...someplace else.

The conversation moved on as we continued eating. The burgers were really good, but greasy, and the oils got ingrained in my hands. A simple napkin wouldn't do the trick. I excused myself to wash up. On my way back from the restroom, I ran into Brittany, who'd been waiting for me in the tiny hallway.

The scar by her eyebrow was defined, so she hadn't come to sneak a kiss in the shadows.

"Should we leave the winery?" she asked.

"Um." I tried to process all the possible meanings her words could take. "I don't think the police would like us to all go home. They might make things difficult."

The scar deepened. "I want to leave because things got difficult."

"This is about Paul, right?" I glanced at our table, my eyes briefly locking with Paul's. Did he know we were talking about him?

Britt said, "I just don't want him in another upsetting environment."

Running a hand through my hair, I thought it through, then sighed. All Britt wanted was to protect her brother. How was I supposed to argue with that? "We could find a nearby hotel or maybe a rental home," I suggested, trying to calculate how much that would cost.

Some of the tension left Britt. "That could work."

"Sure it could." I opened my arms and tried to give a *supportive boyfriend hug*, while wondering if I'd be expected to pay for everyone's rooms.

Glancing at our table, I saw that Paul was no longer watching us, but Juniper was. I expected she'd make childish kissy faces since she'd caught me hugging my girlfriend. Instead, her face remained blank and unreadable. What was up with her? I must've tensed because the next instant Britt was pulling back and staring at my face. "Are you all right?"

"Just great."

Not wanting to have a heart-to-heart by the bathroom, I grabbed her hand and we returned to the table. Suddenly I was exhausted, and we still had to find a new place to stay for the night. The only silver lining was I wouldn't be sleeping under a unicorn princess comforter.

At the table, Brittany announced that *we* had decided it would be best to find somewhere else to stay. It was the first time Britt had said *we* had decided anything. Should that be exciting? But all I could think of was trying not to squirm or fidget as everyone looked at the two of us after Britt's announcement.

I wasn't quite sure who had spoken last, but it was apparently my turn to say something. "Um, yeah."

I'm a fantastic boyfriend.

Juniper started to ask, "Why would—"

But one meaningful head tilt from Britt toward Paul had Juniper and Sienna agreeing with what *we* had decided.

Paul's not an idiot.

I'm sure he caught on to all the concerned glances being shot his way since the police arrived. A frustrated smile played at his lips, and it took him a long time to figure out what to say. "Why would we leave our free rooms to pay for a hotel?"

It was one of those times when everyone at the table answered at once, and every single answer was bad.

I said, "Unicorns."

Juniper said, "Bad lighting."

Sienna said, "No reason."

And Britt said, "Bed bugs."

The tension in Paul's face remained for half a second before he burst out laughing. "Do you hear yourselves? Holt, if the unicorn comforter is such a big deal, we can switch beds. Juniper, I saw some of the precious moments you've recorded, and the lighting was perfect. Now, Sienna"—he took his girlfriend's hand—"if there really is *no reason* to leave, we might as well stay. And, Brittany"—he let out a sigh, his affection for his sister obvious—"what makes you think the room has bed bugs?"

No one was volunteering to answer Paul, so after waiting a couple of beats he continued. "If the only reason is to protect me from reliving stuff from my past, don't worry about it."

Britt and Sienna both opened their mouths, ready to argue, but he was too quick for them. "If anything, I'd worry about Holt. He's the one who found her."

That was a low blow. In a moment the attention shifted from Paul to me. I had to think fast. Smoothing out my hair, I asked, "Were you serious about sleeping on the unicorn bed?"

That cut the tension, and they all laughed. Unfortunately, Paul didn't clarify whether or not I could sleep on the bed with the rocket ships. At least it was decided we'd be staying at the winery, so I wouldn't be footing the bill for lodging five adults and one dog.

On the ride back to Rose's Vineyard, Brittany gave up her permanent right to shotgun so Paul wouldn't be cramped in the car's back seat. I tried to catch her eye through the rearview mirror, but Britt was too busy chatting with Sienna to notice. Every time I glanced at the mirror, it was Juniper who was staring at me. I wanted to twist around and tell her to cut it out, but with my girlfriend and her family in the car, I remained on my best behavior.

For the most part, I was able to ignore Juniper and was contemplating another shower as I pulled into the parking lot. Before I could even unbuckle my seat belt, Juniper was leaning between the seats and telling me to "Wait a minute."

Britt shot me a quizzical look, and I shrugged. I would never dream of suggesting I could read Juniper's mind, but she'd been behaving extra weirdly since the police questioned us.

Once the car had emptied, Juniper took the vacant shotgun seat. She didn't speak, but her nose was all scrunched up. If I didn't know any better, I'd say she was nervous. But if my sister was ever nervous, she'd grown out of that by age three.

I waited for her to say something, waited and waited. I tried to be patient. I'm obviously an extremely patient person. Still, there's only so long a man can wait for his cryptic sister to start talking.

Could I just leave? Say, *sorry, time's up* and go upstairs?

My hand was on the door when Juniper decided to open her mouth. "I need you to tell me the truth."

Strange. In general, I don't make a habit of lying.

I rolled my eyes. "Okayyy."

Juniper twisted in the seat to face me but wouldn't meet my eyes. Her face was pinkish, like she had a fever. After she took a deep breath, her question came out in a rush. "Why did you lie to the cops?"

I'd done what now?

CHAPTER 3

"Are you kidding me?" I said. "This is why I ditched Brittany?" I left the car immediately, so annoyed with myself for getting dragged into one of Juniper's conspiracies.

"Holt." Juniper managed to run in front of me, blocking my progress. "Whatever happened, you can tell me. That's why I waited until we were alone."

My temples began to burn, and I took a step back. All the playfulness had left my sister's face, and she seemed worried. I still had no clue what she was upset about, but whatever it was, she was definitely concerned.

I took a deep breath, trying to refocus on the moment. "I don't lie to the police."

Juniper stepped close, her voice low. "Then why did you tell them you didn't know Natasha Ryan?"

"Because I don't!" My voice was raised, and I lowered it as I said, "Her falling into my arms doesn't count as an introduction."

Juniper tilted her head, taking her time studying my face. "You really don't know?"

This was getting ridiculous. "Know what?"

"Natasha was your college girlfriend."

College girlfriend? The only real college girlfriend I'd had was...

"Tasha?"

Juniper nodded. "Tasha *is* Natasha."

Without much grace, I sat on the curb. I remembered Tasha. Not that it mattered, but she was my longest relationship.

"See." Juniper had joined me on the curb and was shoving her phone in my face. There was a picture about a decade old of me and Tasha.

This wasn't the point of the pic, but my hair and clothes weren't doing me any favors. It's not that I looked bad in college, but I'd prefer Britt not see the photos from that time. I'd grown my hair down to my shoulders and wore a braided necklace Tasha had given me. Which is fine. A different style from now, but it was college.

The real problem was that in every casual photo from the time, I was wearing an unzipped sweatshirt with no shirt on underneath. Ever since I started regular ab workouts as a teen, I've had great abs. The problem is the guy in those photos looks like a real jerk, like a villain in a kids' movie.

Then there was Tasha. She was crooked in my arm, smirking at the camera with her lip piercings and blue-black hair.

I pushed Juniper's arm away. "I remember what my ex-girlfriend looks like."

Juniper's lips pressed together. "Are you sure you know what Tasha looks like?" She exited out of the photo to show Tasha's Facebook profile, and with a few swipes of her fingers, the images changed, the hair becoming a natural light brown, and the lip piercings disappearing, until the woman who'd fallen into my arms emerged.

That woman was Tasha? I accidentally swallowed air and then began coughing.

"Are you okay?" Juniper put a hand on my back.

I shifted away from her. "No, I'm not okay. I just found out that..."

What had I found out? Who was Tasha to me now?

I shook my head. "I just found out...I lied to the cops."

"That's why you're freaking out?" Juniper asked.

"Accidentally lying to police during a murder investigation seems like a pretty good reason."

And really, how was I supposed to explain to the police that I hadn't recognized my ex-girlfriend?

What were the chances we'd be reunited for her murder? Would the police believe my story? What would Brittany think? What would I think if the roles were reversed?

I needed to tell the police right away. They'd cleared out of Rose's Vineyard while we were eating, so I called the non-emergency line. After a series of transfers and being put on hold, I reached an annoyed voice, who told me to expect an officer in twenty minutes.

Juniper stayed on the curb while I paced the sidewalk, trying not to pull my hair out.

Had Tasha known who I was? Unbidden, my brain replayed what she'd said when she'd stumbled toward me. Originally I'd guessed she'd been asking for help. But Tasha hadn't asked for *help*. She'd been saying *Holt*. Almost dead, she knew exactly who I was, and I'd treated her like a stranger.

Though I'd probably be spared from this whole mess if she hadn't stopped dyeing her hair blue. Would the police believe me if I blamed my lack of recognition on a dye job?

This wasn't good.

Then I remembered my buddy Darren's a lawyer. It wouldn't hurt to call him. A part of me hoped he wouldn't answer. The whole thing was so embarrassing. Besides, I don't think Darren's ever done criminal law, so what would he know?

"How's my favorite wino doing?" Darren asked as a greeting.

How was I friends with this person?

"Evening" was all he got from me before I launched into the reason for my call. "So, hypothetically, how much trouble would someone be in if he originally told police officers he didn't recognize a murder victim only to find out later it was his ex-girlfriend?"

At first the line was so silent I checked to make sure the call hadn't dropped. Then I heard garbled words, like Darren was covering the speaker and letting off some steam. Finally he was on the line, sounding his most professional. "Holt, this is very serious. You need to tell the police immediately."

I sighed, realizing I'd wanted Darren to laugh and say it was no big deal. "I know," I said. "They're on their way."

"Good. Apologize and do your best to explain what happened."

"Yeah, thanks." Running my free hand through my hair, I said, "You know, I really didn't recognize her."

Darren barked a laugh. "The sad part is, I believe you."

After we hung up, I didn't have long to wait for an unmarked car to pull up. Instead of twenty minutes, a police officer was here in closer to ten.

When Cop Kid got out of the car, he gave me and Juniper a curious look. "You're here?"

I nodded. What had he expected? I'd request an interview and then wander off into the grapevines?

"Well, let's head in." He led the way inside. As we walked, he kept turning around to look at me, a curious expression on his face. It was like he was two seconds away from asking a question, yet the words never came.

Brittany had been waiting in the lobby, and her face mirrored the cop's confusion as we passed her.

Oh no.

Brittany.

It was bad enough explaining to the cops my ex-girlfriend had the bizarre timing of dying in my arms, but what was I supposed to tell Brittany? Worst-case scenario, all the police would do was arrest me for murder. But Brittany might dump me.

All I could do was nod an acknowledgment at Britt before following the cop upstairs. Cop Kid, Juniper, and I all ended up in the same second-floor bedroom where they'd previously held interviews.

The cop raised his eyebrows when he saw Juniper had followed us into the temporary interrogation room. Turned out she wasn't officially invited to this little party. Still, this cop looked like he was twelve years old, and there are many adults who can't turn down my sister with her doe eyes.

"So, Holt," Cop Kid said, choosing to ignore my sister. "Once I got back to the station, I called to notify Natasha's adoptive parents. After I notified them of her death, they gave me an overview of Tasha's life, including her ex-boyfriends. One name stood out."

Wait. This couldn't be happening. How had Tasha's parents even remembered me? It wasn't like we'd ever met. Now Cop Kid would think I was hiding my relationship with Tasha, but I'd literally called the police the moment I'd found I dated her.

"Can you guess what name stood out?" Cop Kid asked.

"Yeah," I said, gripping the edge of the table. "It was mine. Her parents said, *Tasha dated Holt Jacobs in college*."

"That's correct." There was an undercurrent of menace in his voice. "Now, this evening when we asked if you knew her, you said no. So you can understand my confusion when I found out you'd dated for a year."

"It wasn't that long."

Juniper kicked me under the table.

Fine. I wouldn't argue about how many months Tasha and I had or hadn't dated. "Sorry," I muttered. Then I took a deep breath and tried again. "I know how this must look, but I didn't recognize her."

Cop Kid made a sound that was part snort and part laugh. "Excuse me?" he asked after he'd recovered.

Right. Time to clear up I wasn't a liar.

"My sister…" Was it bad I'd brought Juniper into this? Would that make her an accomplice? "Or, um, Juniper, upon further consideration, did some investigating and figured out who Tasha was."

Cop Kid had been jotting down notes, but at this his pen stopped and he side-eyed Juniper, with a *Is this guy serious?* face.

"We dated, like, ten years ago," I said. Then, when the detective still made no comment, I added, "Her hair was dyed blue and she had lip rings. Tasha looked nothing like Natasha Ryan."

The cop carefully placed the pen in the notebook and folded his hands on the table. "But she has the same name. Why didn't you recognize that?"

I sighed, knowing the truth sounded dumb. "I'm really bad with names."

"That's true," Juniper added. The officer shot her a warning glare.

I tapped my fingers on the table, trying to think of a decent explanation. "My ex's name was Tasha. Facebook was the main social media when we dated. She put *Tasha* for her first name and *Natasha* as her last name." I shook my head, desperate for him to believe me. "I didn't know anyone named Natasha Ryan. And the woman who fell into my arms wasn't someone I recognized."

The cop began nodding slowly. It was probably meant to be soothing, but I could see the shift in his mind as I became his top suspect.

"I didn't know who she was," I said, feeling a cold sweat forming. I was really done with people thinking I was a murderer. It had happened enough this year.

"Don't worry, Mr. Jacobs. I'll look into it," Cop Kid said, managing a perfectly professional voice.

Right. I was clearly in good hands.

"You have to believe him," Juniper said, leaning across the table and clasping Cop Kid's hands in hers. "Please."

My sister can have quite the effect on men, and this guy was no different. He stared at her, his mouth agape.

When he was finally able to pull his hands free of Juniper, he began fiddling with his notebook. "As I said, I'll look into it. Let us know if any new information comes to light." And with that, he practically ran from the room.

I bumped Juniper's shoulder. "Look what you did to the poor guy."

Juniper shrugged. "He'll be fine. He needed to remember you're an innocent bystander."

"That's not what he'll remember."

"Eh, I tried."

In the hallway, I closed the bedroom door, and the automatic lock clicked into place. Juniper headed for the stairs but turned around when I didn't follow. "You coming?"

Of course I was. Any moment I'd start moving. But I wasn't looking forward to going upstairs and explaining myself to Britt. Why couldn't I just go to bed?

Wait. Bed. Looking at the locked bedroom the police had been using, I remembered the very normal maroon comforter on the bed. Juniper read my thoughts. "Too bad you can't get in. Otherwise you could add stealing a comforter to your list of crimes."

I knew the door was locked, but I double-checked the handle just in case.

Juniper came to stand beside the door. "Think about it. Your bed's a twin. That one's a queen. The blanket would drag on the floor. Now, let's go."

We were headed to the third floor when a commotion downstairs had the ever-curious Juniper leading us all the way back down to the ground floor.

In the lobby, Cop Kid was talking to a couple of uniformed officers. Seeing us, our cop tilted his head for us to join their group.

"These officers said you called with new information."

Which officers?

"Umm, yeah, I called," I said, not understanding all the confused faces. "I called the station as soon as I realized who Tasha was."

Cop Kid frowned. "You called?"

"Right away," Juniper said for me. "Show him your phone."

I did as my sister suggested, and a few seconds later Cop Kid was looking at my call history. Then he turned to the officers. "Thanks for coming out," he said, and he shook their hands. "There was a miscommunication, and I already took Mr. Jacobs's statement." He waited for the officers to leave before saying, "Next time you have any revelations about the case, call me directly." Cop Kid handed me a business card. Then he turned away quickly. I couldn't see his face, but I could swear he was enjoying this.

"Will do," I said.

With his back still turned, he said, "Thanks for your statement, and have a good night." Then he left.

Before I had a moment to breathe, Juniper grabbed my phone.

"What are you doing?" I asked, making a half-hearted attempt to get my phone back. The screen was still unlocked, and with Juniper, you never know what trick she might try out.

Juniper began tapping on the screen. "I'm adding his number to your contacts so you can give him a call before you do something stupid."

"You're wasting your time," I said. "I never do anything stupid."

Juniper rolled her eyes. "Then you're too stupid to know what the word *stupid* means." She handed me the phone and went upstairs.

I followed Juniper at a slower speed. While I should have used that time to figure out the best way to explain myself to Brittany, I really spent it wondering whether Paul would let me sleep on the rocket ship bed.

When I got to our suite, Juniper was on her phone, already settled on the sectional next to Sienna and Paul. Britt wasn't there, but the light to the girls' room was on and the door was ajar.

How bad of a boyfriend would I be if I went to bed without explaining my second interview to the cops or even saying good night? The problem was Brittany's a cool enough person she'd understand. She'd let me off the hook because of what I'd gone through.

I couldn't give Britt another opportunity to prove how great she was. So I knocked lightly on the door.

"Come in," she said, setting down her e-reader as I entered. The girls' room was a lot nicer than the one I was bunking in with Paul. There was a queen-size bed with a trundle bed partially pulled out underneath, plus a love seat, which Britt was currently curled up on.

When my eyes lingered on the room, Britt said, "I didn't choose the room assignments." At least there was a hint of humor in her voice.

Sitting next to her on the love seat, I tried to grin. "And if it were your choice, you would have gone with pink unicorn castles?"

Britt's lips twitched. "You know how much I love pink unicorn castles."

I stifled a yawn. "I'll need to remember that for Christmas."

Had I just mentioned Christmas? A holiday that was three months away? This was bad. Britt's scar by her eyebrow was visible. I'd been presumptuous and freaked her out. What was I thinking?

"You look tired," Britt said.

Wait. Was that why she was worried? Not about my Christmas comment? Shifting on the love seat to face her, I said, "It's been a long day."

Brittany gave a mock frown. "The day's not over yet. Do you want to know what time it is?"

"No, I don't."

She hadn't lived in Seattle for very long, but already it was clear I could fall asleep during a ten-minute car ride, while Britt would stay awake during horrendously long and boring movies. I guess it was a good thing. You want your first responders to be alert anytime, day or night.

Resting my head back, I closed my eyes. "It's mostly dark outside, which is late enough for me."

I could have fallen asleep like that and was beginning to drift when Britt's quiet "Holt" left me peeking an eye open.

"Yeah?"

"Was there a reason you came to my room? Something you wanted to tell me about the police coming back?"

Oh. That whole *I had to tell the cops I didn't recognize my ex-girlfriend when she died in my arms.*

I sat up and rubbed my face in my hands, trying to wake up. Time to have an adult conversation.

"So, I think I've mentioned my college girlfriend."

"Tasha, the psych major?" Britt asked.

"Yeah, her."

Brittany knew her name? How had she remembered that? It wasn't like I was someone who spent hours a week crying to his current girlfriend about women from his past.

"Um, well. Tasha is Natasha Ryan."

"I see." Brittany's response was so unreactive, I wondered if she hadn't understood.

Should I rephrase?

What else could I say?

I added, "The woman who died."

Britt tilted her head. "So, you didn't recognize the only real girlfriend you've ever had?"

"Uh, yeah."

So she had understood...Yay?

"Was that all you wanted to say?" Brittany's face was impassive, and she was using her paramedic voice.

"That's it," I answered. But all I wanted was to know what she was thinking.

"Well, thank you for letting me know." Brittany stood and offered me a hand up before placing a kiss on my cheek.

My cheek—not my mouth.

I swallowed down a yawn before asking, "Am I in trouble?"

"Holt..." Britt reconsidered what she'd been about to say. "We've both had long days, and you're about sixty seconds away from crashing. Let's talk about this tomorrow."

She hadn't answered my question, so the answer was, yes, I was in trouble.

Why did Tasha have to remove her piercings and change her hair? If she'd looked the same, it would have saved me a lot of trouble with the police and my girlfriend.

"Holt?"

Was I still in Britt's room? "Yeah?"

"Go to bed."

I didn't need to be told again. So I gave Brittany a quick kiss on the mouth and was relieved when she didn't pull away. Then I left. Funny, I was almost looking forward to sleeping under my pink unicorn bedspread.

But here's the thing about Juniper, she's crafty. While I'd grown semi-accustomed to the idea of my princess comforter, I hadn't bothered checking the mattress until I was finally tumbling into bed. It crinkled. Everything beneath me crinkled.

At first I was too tired to understand what felt like a tarp between the sheet and the mattress was more or less what it was. Peeling off the corner of the fitted sheet, I found a mattress protector—the kind that soaks up leaks from little kids who pee in the middle of the night.

Juniper was going to give me gray hairs.

There was a snuffling by my door, followed by a "shush." I knew at that moment Juniper was listening by the door and Chouzie had joined her.

I was too tired to give Juniper the satisfaction of a temper tantrum. She could wait all night if she wanted, but I wouldn't get out of bed to complain, and I definitely wasn't removing the protector. No way was I taking off the comforter and sheets to unzip the pee protector and somehow wriggle it off the mattress. That was wayyy too much work.

I kept the lamp on for Paul. The light wouldn't affect my sleep, though the crinkling sheet might...

Pulling the unicorn blanket above my shoulders, I let myself relax.

Whatever Juniper's plans for my night were, she couldn't have known the biggest disrupter to my sleep wouldn't be the pee protection or the pink bedding. It was sharing a room with Paul. The man might be unfairly attractive, but he had some messed-up nasal passages and snored at a disjointed rhythm and tempo. It was early, early morning when the sound first broke through my sleep. I thought I would get used to it, but in the end I got up before 5:00 a.m.

By the time I abandoned our bedroom, I was too cranky to fall back asleep on the couch. I glanced at the girls' bedroom. Paul and Brittany were twins. Was horrible snoring genetic? For a moment I considered listening by their door, but that was too creepy for so early in the morning.

I took a quick shower, then hunted in our main room's kitchenette for a coffeepot. There was a Keurig under the kitchenette's sink, but I couldn't find any K-Cups. Dressed in a pair of joggers and a pullover, I went down to the ground floor in search of coffee.

The front rooms were dim, but there was the soft clatter of someone working in the kitchen. I headed toward the sounds. I'm not exactly cheerful first thing in the morning, but when coffee's at stake, I'm willing to do almost anything. If I had to muster a smile and make small talk, so be it.

The kitchen had one of those doors that swung both ways. I gave a quick knock before entering—in general I find it best not to scare people who may be wielding butcher knives.

Quirky Sue was pouring out muffin batter, her hair pulled back into tight little pigtails. "Good morning," she said.

"Morning."

How much chitchat was necessary before I could get the coffee?

"Did you sleep okay?" she asked.

Maybe it was all in my head, but Quirky Sue's ears were turning pink, and I got the suspicion Juniper had told everyone at Rose's Vineyard that I needed a mattress protector. And really, if I had that problem, (which I don't), I would just get diapers instead of confiding such problems to hospitality workers.

Coffee was momentarily forgotten. I had an image to keep up.

Leaning against the counter, I gave my best lazy smile. "I slept great. I was surprised how comfortable the trundle bed was, and I'm sure Juniper's loving the pink unicorn bed."

"Juniper?" Quirky Sue's ears turned from pink to red.

My beloved sister had definitely *confided* my supposed secret.

I dug Juniper's grave a little deeper. "Yes. That bed was for Juniper." I grinned. "Did she say it was for someone else? She can be so shy about her...love of unicorns."

"Uh-huh," Quirky Sue said, concentrating extra hard on the muffin batter.

With my host feeling sufficiently uncomfortable, I got down to business. "So I found a Keurig in the room but didn't see any K-Cups."

"Oh, sorry." Sue looked sad. Why was she sad about K-Cups? "That was Rose's job. She always did the final checks."

"Rose?" I asked. If yesterday was any indicator, I'm not exactly great with names. But with Rose's name plastered everywhere, you'd think I'd remember meeting her. Was she the fifth person with glasses from the photos?

When the muffins were put in the oven and Quirky Sue faced me again, the sadness was gone. "The vineyard, buildings, everything—it was all Rose's. The five of us met in college in the nineties and have stayed together ever since."

She'd said *was*. Rose *was* the owner. Had Rose died or sold the property?

"What happened to her?" I asked.

Quirky Sue's eyes watered. "She recently passed away." Her voice trembled as she spoke. "Rose knew about her heart disease for a while, so it was sort of expected. Still"—her voice broke—"I just can't believe she's gone." Then Quirky Sue started crying, and I wanted to bang my head against a wall.

Why had I asked about Rose? I should have gotten my coffee and left.

Now that I'd have to wait for her to calm down before I could get my caffeine, I set a tentative hand on her shoulder. "I'm sorry," I said in a low tone that was meant to be soothing.

Unfortunately, this just made Quirky Sue cry harder, and before I knew it, she was clinging to me. Was she getting snot and tears on my pullover?

Gingerly, I lifted my arms and did my best to pat her back. I kept saying, "Shhhh. Shhh." But I don't think Quirky Sue had any idea how much I really wanted her to shut up.

Rose was dead. Strangely, that information left me a little sad. Of anyone at the winery, she seemed like the one who got things done.

The awkwardness from last night's tasting made more sense. Everything at Rose's Vineyard had been under Rose's care. She made sure the tastings went smoothly. She made sure there were K-Cups in the rooms. How many jobs had slipped since her passing? And problems in the winery's upkeep probably started while she was still alive but growing too sick to handle the winery's operations.

Was this the reason Juniper was invited to the winery? The managers needed something to encourage customers to return after the loss of the company's leading force?

There was a flash of movement by the door, and Britt entered. Our eyes met, mine panicked, hers surprised and then amused. I tilted my head, beckoning her into the room. But her mouth quirked, and after a moment's hesitation, Britt left me alone with the crying woman. Was this punishment for forgetting Tasha?

I don't know how long I was stuck in the kitchen with the sobbing woman or how much longer we would have stayed like that if a timer hadn't gone off.

Sue went off to check the oven, and I debated leaving the kitchen. But coffee. I really love coffee. If I left the winery, it would be a bit of a drive to find a place that was open.

Thankfully, once Quirky Sue was done with the oven, she acted like nothing had happened, which worked for me. She led me over to a cupboard, where she let me pick from a variety of K-Cups.

Personally, I would have gone for nothing but caffeinated coffee, but Britt's a tea drinker—I only discovered this flaw after I'd known her for weeks and was too far gone to hold it against her. So, while I loaded up on coffee, I also got tea for Brittany. Though after she'd ditched me with a weeping woman, she was lucky I was so kind.

On my way back, I paused to look at the photos in the main room. From the pictures, they proclaimed themselves to be the perfect friend group. Rose was in the center of most of the photos, and I wouldn't say it was a huge leap to assume she controlled the group.

From Quirky Sue's comment about Rose owning everything and doing the final inspections, it sounded like Rose had been the only one in charge. And she'd definitely used her name in all the branding.

At last night's tasting, I kept feeling someone was missing. Was Rose such a part of the winery that it barely functioned without her? How had things changed since Rose's death? She'd known about her heart disease for a while. Surely Rose would have made a will with some clear arrangements.

Could that be a factor in Tasha's murder? Was it coincidental Rose died of heart failure and not long after that Tasha had shown up at the vineyard, supposedly knowing no one before getting murdered?

Was it crazier to believe Rose's and Tasha's deaths were connected or that the deaths were a coincidence?

Chapter 4

A crash from the kitchen reminded me I was still downstairs with absolutely no coffee in my system, so I headed upstairs. Why was I so drawn to those photos? Something about Rose's face stuck with me.

When I got back to the suite, Britt was in the shower and nobody else was up. I made myself the inaugural first cup of coffee, then made Britt a cup of tea.

Checking my phone, I found an alarming number of texts on the family group chat. Usually it happened when my niece or nephew did something *impressive* or Juniper was pretending to be modest.

But instead of a photo featuring a family member, Juniper had sent a candid shot of me. And I mean *very* candid. Last night, after I'd fallen asleep, she'd snuck into my room and taken a picture of me wrapped up in that infernal pink comforter.

My movie-star looks had vanished, replaced by a slack jaw, and I was drooling onto a unicorn. Unfortunately, my family loved it. There were tons of comments and GIFs that only fed the monster that is Juniper. She then sent pictures of me sleeping on random other vacations, and the cycle continued.

Mom had texted me privately asking me to call her, but the funny thing about my parents having a midlife crisis and moving to Australia was that she was in a drastically different time zone. It was kind of confusing. Australia's nineteen hours ahead, which really meant she was five hours behind me for clock time, except she was living in the future.

So weird.

I sent Mom an *I'm alive* text—deciding to leave out that I'd neither killed Juniper nor sued her for defamation of character. After pressing send, I wondered if I should tell Mom about Tasha. They'd never met, yet Mom had a way of sensing when I was in trouble.

Darren had also texted: *What happened?*

I'd kind of forgotten I'd called my friend for some free legal counsel.

Darren hadn't forgotten. And he hadn't given up after one text. Twenty minutes later Darren had sent: *Were you arrested?*

There was also a missed call with no voicemail. Then (and this proves how awful my baby sister truly is) Darren had forwarded the photo of me sleeping on the unicorn bedding.

Darren: *Glad to know you're alive.*

What? He'd contacted my sister?

The moment I saw the pic, I was texting my reply: *You'd better delete that photo.*

Immediately my phone lit up with an incoming call from Darren.

Gross. I wasn't ready to talk to more people. But I couldn't let it go to voicemail since Darren knew I was by my phone.

Since it was a Friday morning he'd be exercising before going to work. He'd be way too energetic. The phone kept vibrating while I hesitated. The call was about to drop when I answered.

"Hello?"

"Can you guess how long it took me to remember I had Juniper's number saved in my phone?" Darren didn't bother with any pleas-antries.

I stayed silent since the question seemed more rhetorical. So for a few seconds there was nothing but the sound of exercise machines whirring from his side of the call.

Darren sighed. "Juniper told me everything was fine. Is that correct?"

"Mostly fine," I said.

"Well, that's good, I guess. Next time you call me for pro bono legal advice, you have to keep me updated."

"Next time?" I asked. "Why do you assume there's going to be a next time?"

Darren chuckled. "Oh, there's definitely going to be a next time."

"Fine," I said, since he was probably right. "What if *next time*, instead of having to remember to give you an update, I just pay you for your services?"

"You'd rather pay my hourly?" Darren asked, and it sounded like a challenge.

"If it saves me a phone call," I said.

Darren muttered something I couldn't hear, but his mood seemed to be improving when he said, "All right, pay me next time. But you should know I charge for time spent *thinking* about my clients. So I would bill for most of last night."

Before I could answer, there was the low creaking of a door being opened. I was so excited Britt was out of the shower, I didn't even check to make sure it was her.

"Sorry, man, I gotta go," I said.

"Keep me updated," Darren said as I was hanging up.

But I could have kept talking to Darren, because it wasn't my girlfriend. It was my sister.

Even a little fuzzy around the edges, Juniper looked ready for a photo shoot. And from the pic she'd shared with the family, it was clear I took work to be attractive.

Juniper sat right beside me and rested her head on my shoulder.

"Did you sleep okay?" I asked.

"Uh-huh." Juniper was quiet, then sat up quickly as she remembered her own shenanigans. "What about you? How was the mattress?"

My jaw ticked. I hated the potty-proof mattress, but letting Juniper know would only encourage her. I shrugged. "You know I'm fine. A bed's a bed."

"Okay." Juniper didn't sound disappointed. Maybe I hadn't played my role convincingly. "And have you checked your phone?" she asked.

"Yup."

"And what did you think?"

I took a long drink of coffee. "I have no thoughts."

"Holt." Juniper swatted my arm. It was amazing how quickly she became alert. Already she was more awake than me, and she hadn't touched a drop of caffeine. "You need to have thoughts. This involves you."

"Hardly," I muttered.

Juniper studied my face. "Are you serious?" she asked. "You weren't going to reply to the group chat?"

I set my mug down with more force than intended. "And what would I say? *LOL*, with a laughing emoji?"

"What?" Juniper's brow wrinkled, and she seemed genuinely confused. Maybe she wasn't alert, just energetic. "Oh." A faint blush tinted her cheeks. "Not the photo. I sent that, didn't I? Sorry, that last glass of wine was a bad call."

I raised an eyebrow. "The photo was an accident?"

"Sort of."

"What about the pink comforter and the pee protector?"

Juniper giggled. "Those were completely on purpose."

"That's what I thought." I shifted away from Juniper, but she scooted even closer. Apparently, I wasn't allowed to be mad at her, so I drank more coffee.

"But what about the other thing?" Juniper asked.

"The other photos you sent? I've seen most of them before."

Juniper huffed out a breath like I was being intentionally difficult. "I'm not talking about my texts. I'm talking about Mom's."

"Mom's?"

"Wait. You didn't read it?"

I'm not exactly one hundred percent at reading the group chat. And the amount I read decreases the more I'm being teased.

Juniper sighed. "Holt, Mom sent this long message about us all spending Christmas together."

I raised an eyebrow. "Does Mom really expect us all to fly out to Australia?"

The time change would kill me. Like, literally kill me. And if by some miracle I survived, I'd get acclimated just in time for the return trip to Seattle, only to be killed by another time change.

"Not Australia," Juniper said, tapping at her phone screen. She handed me the phone, where a message from Mom was pulled up.

While the text was long and contained a lot of unnecessary details, the basics were Mom and Dad would be in the States for Christmas. Mom was planning on renting a large vacation home and wanted a head count so she'd know how many beds were needed.

Christmas? It was mid-September and I needed to decide whether I wanted to join a family pressure cooker for Christmas? As much as

I loved my family, my time wasn't my own on these trips. Mom had strict schedules. Plus, Casey's kids are loud.

"Are you all right?" Juniper laughed. "Your face is green."

I cleared my throat. "This is my excited face."

"So you'll go?"

I let out a long sigh. "If I remember correctly, I said no to the last family trip, and then you and Mom guilted me into going anyway."

Juniper tried to look innocent. "Does that really sound like us?"

I leveled her with a glare, and she giggled.

The bathroom door opened, and Britt appeared in a bathrobe with damp hair. I was immediately on my feet. "Morning," I said.

Her face remained neutral as she said, "Good morning." Before I could say anything else, she disappeared into the girls' room.

It wasn't ideal.

"You'll be fine," Juniper said, coming to stand beside me. "Just give her some time to process how you could completely forget about Tasha—someone who once meant the world to you."

I frowned at Juniper.

She smiled. "There he is. Now, come on. I have to take Chouzie for a walk. You shouldn't be moping around all day."

"Britt will be upset all day?"

"How would I know?"

It wasn't until the three of us were almost out the door that I froze. I was still in the joggers I'd slept in, and Juniper had just rolled out of bed. "Don't you want to...freshen up?"

Juniper hadn't set foot in the rest room, and the sweatshirt she wore was one of her husband's and was really baggy on her.

Juniper tossed her hair. "Why would I?" she asked, and left our suite.

That was confidence.

I'd assumed it was a simple walk outside to give Chouzie a chance to do his business. While that did happen, Juniper then set off between the grapevines toward the distant sound of workers harvesting.

"Someone here knew Tasha," I said, stopping in the middle of a row of grapes.

Juniper tapped a finger on her lips, pretending to think, before saying, "*Someone* did know her."

I rolled my eyes. "Besides me. Someone had to know her to have killed her."

"Maybe." Juniper scrunched up her nose. "Wasn't she inside the winery?"

"Yes."

"Maybe she was a stranger but was murdered because she'd discovered a secret."

"Sure," I said. "Tasha discovered their fermentation secrets."

Juniper shoved my shoulder. "I'm not saying I know the secret. I'm saying there could be a secret."

"That's what I just said."

"Well"—Juniper resumed walking—"I said it differently."

Hard to argue with that.

What sort of secrets are common in wineries, and how easy are they to discover? Could I discover any by walking through the space?

"Do you know if the whole winery's a crime scene?" I asked.

"Let's see." Juniper wrinkled her nose. "I'm pretty sure I heard Brad going over which sections they were still authorized to use. So I guess only parts of the building are closed off."

"Can you get us into the winery?" I asked, since it was so much easier to snoop when you weren't breaking and entering. "Like, say you need a tour?"

"Hmm?" Juniper tugged at Chouzie's leash when the chow chow became overly enamored with a twig. "Oh. Probably." Juniper flashed an influencer smile. "I'll tell them it'll help with their branding if I get some videos of the fermentation process."

We reached a slight vista, and the vineyard stretched out in front of us. In the distance were low hills with scrubby bushes.

Juniper took a deep breath. "Hard to put a price on this." Without missing a beat, she took out her phone and reenacted the same moment for the camera. And supposedly people liked my sister's content because it was organic.

When the camera was off, Juniper tapped a finger to her lips. "Honestly I'm not sure why they're having trouble booking this place. Rose's Vineyard should sell itself."

I shook my head. "But it's not Rose's anymore." Something clicked in my brain. "Juniper, did their occupancy start decreasing in the last few months?"

"How should I know?"

"Well, what reasons did they give you for coming to the winery?"

Juniper shrugged. "I didn't question the *all-expenses-paid trip* I was invited on."

Of course she didn't. Why would she? Why not assume everything would work out in a picture-perfect world?

"About that," I said, since Juniper bringing up the *all-expenses-paid trip* was the best opening I could hope for. "Is this really all free?"

"Excuse me?" Juniper asked as we turned around and began our return trip back to the buildings of Rose's Vineyard.

"You've said *all expenses*, but are they really giving us all free food, wine, and housing?"

Juniper stopped, crossed her arms, and popped her hip. "No, they're not just giving it to us for free."

I knew it. I knew there had to be some catch.

She pointed a finger in my face. "Don't get so excited. What I meant is they're paying me room and board for all the exposure they get from having me and Chouzie here."

"And that's really the deal?" I asked.

Juniper rolled her eyes. "You can read the contract, but I had my lawyer look over it, and he said the arrangement was perfectly fine."

Lawyer? My sister has a lawyer?

I must've looked skeptical because Juniper raised her head high and said, "Just because I don't have a job where my employer is contributing money to my 401k doesn't mean I don't take my work seriously."

"Work? Juniper, your job is having fun on camera."

"Sure. That's all I do," Juniper said, then stormed off.

I had to jog a few steps to catch up. "Hey, come on. I'm sorry," I said.

But Juniper didn't slow down.

"You know I'm a boring old man who likes a steady job with benefits."

"You are old," Juniper said, beginning to soften.

"That's the spirit." I grinned. "And I'm sorry if I downplayed your entrepreneurial accomplishments. I just didn't remember you mentioning anything like this happening before."

"Oh." Juniper didn't say anything else, but her cheeks turned pink and she began biting her lip.

What was she hiding?

"Juniper?"

"Okay, so this is a...unique experience." Juniper quickly added, "But I have been given complimentary things in the past."

"So what I'm hearing is that I was right."

Juniper rolled her eyes. "Not what I said. But I'll admit, it's usually a complimentary facial or a water bottle. I've never been offered something at this scale."

So Juniper had told the truth about the free vacation. But the managers offering Juniper an all-expense-paid trip was definitely fishy.

"What about your social media would make them ask you specifically?" I asked.

Juniper shook her head. "I don't know. The offer came during our Idaho trip. I figured they liked the footage I had with Chouzie."

"So I should be thanking Chouzie for my vacation?" I asked, playfully bumping into Juniper.

"Please do," Juniper said.

"What?"

"I would love to see you thank Chouzie for anything. I won't even film."

"Yeah, I'm not going to thank your dog," I said.

Juniper pouted, but I kept walking.

We passed a sign with a full map of Rose's Vineyard. It reminded me of what Quirky Sue had told me. The vineyard was Rose's. It may have been a group of five friends. They may have all worked here. But it all belonged to Rose. With her gone, who was next in line?

We'd nearly returned to Rose's Repose when Juniper asked, "Will you ask Brittany to come?"

Was Juniper talking about the winery-snooping-tour? I'd been too busy mulling over Rose's succession line. I shrugged. "I don't know if she has any plans for today."

"I meant for Christmas," Juniper said.

Christmas? Invite a woman I wanted to like me on a trip that was a boiling pot of family activities? The thought left me momentarily dizzy.

Juniper was still talking, "...know how Mom is. She'll want to get the head count right away, and..."

Brittany was barely talking to me. How was I supposed to suggest we spend Christmas together? She'd just moved to Seattle, and Christmas was months away. How would that even work? A new wave of dizziness hit when I realized I wanted Britt to come. Sure it sounded like a bad idea, and the list of nightmare outcomes was long, but Britt getting to spend time with my family. Them getting to know her...

"You're smiling," Juniper said, and Chouzie barked in agreement.

"No. I'm not." There had to be something very wrong with me if I actually wanted my girlfriend trapped in a house with my family.

Juniper and I had made it to the front porch, when a raised voice caught our attention. "I know...I know...That is what he said last time."

Juniper made a show of crouching down and creeping to the corner of the house to spy on the person talking before sneaking back. "It's Brad," she stage-whispered.

I could have told her that. Bad Brad's voice matched his looks perfectly.

"...He'll be paid..." Brad said, his voice growing more impatient. "I know what Rose's will said, but the situation has changed...Just tell him I'll be there this afternoon."

Juniper and I were waiting to hear more, when Bad Brad appeared around the corner, putting his phone in a pocket.

We reacted a second too late. Juniper began ruffling Chouzie's fur. "It's like he has a rash from irritation."

Bad Brad was eyeing us suspiciously, so I went along with Juniper's performance. Crouching down, I pretended to see a rash under Chouzie's reddish fur. "Uh-huh," I said, because I literally had no words for pretend dog rashes.

I don't know what Brad thought. But Juniper can give convincing performances. Who knows, maybe Bad Brad bought it. At any rate, he didn't accuse us of eavesdropping.

As he grew closer, his features relaxed. "Breakfast is ready," he said with a wink that was probably meant for Juniper.

We followed him inside. Juniper went upstairs to drop Chouzie off in our suite, while I followed Brad to the dining area. Brittany was there, sharing a table with Paul and Sienna, their plates all filled with food. After a quick good morning, I served myself at the buffet table, before taking the empty seat beside Brittany.

Fixing my hair, I told myself not to be smothering and to keep my pining glances to an absolute minimum. So I concentrated on my food.

"How was your walk?"

Had Brittany just asked me a question? My head snapped up. Britt, Sienna, and Paul were waiting expectantly, so she must have asked.

"Um, good," I said.

There was a matching sparkle in Britt's and Paul's eyes, and I got the uncomfortable impression they were laughing at me. I tried to come up with something else to say. Something interesting. "Chouzie liked...the vineyard."

"That's good," Brittany said.

I nodded. Wondering what was wrong with me and if coffee was the cure.

It was a relief when Juniper joined the table. As much as I wanted to check in with Britt, I couldn't do it over eggs and with an audience.

Juniper had freshened up and dashed on some makeup. "So I talked with Hannah. She said we could get a tour this morning. After that, there's another tasting scheduled during lunch, and then we'll go out to the vineyard and try our hand at picking."

My stomach twisted. I get why the staff of Rose's Vineyard were ignoring the whole *murder* thing, but Tasha had just died and the day was set aside for drinking wine and wandering around grapevines.

"What tour?" Sienna asked.

"Oh, Holt wanted a walk-through of the winery building," Juniper said.

"Did he?" Britt analyzed my face, knowing me well enough to suspect I didn't care about the fermentation process.

"Tasha died there," I said for Britt's ears only.

Brittany nodded.

Could she tell my feelings for Tasha were in the past? The only times I'd thought about Tasha in recent years were with a bruised ego because she'd dumped me. Still, even if I had to explain my need to solve her murder to Britt, someone had to care enough to find out what happened. The police were probably too busy tracking down any motives I might have for killing Tasha. If they used all their manpower trying to prove I was an obsessed stalker, they'd have no time to catch the real killer.

"Wait." I'd been too focused on my little investigation to process everything Juniper had said. "Are we picking grapes?"

"Yup."

"So the vineyard's guests are expected to help with the chores?"

Paul chuckled, Britt squeezed my knee, and Sienna said I should try new things, all while my sister and I never broke eye contact.

When Sienna finished talking, Juniper said, "Yes. They expect us to work in the fields."

"It's supposed to make the wine taste better when you appreciate the work that went into it," Paul said, his eyes twinkling.

"I appreciated it just fine last night," I grumbled into my plate.

Average Joe came to our table dressed in work clothes. "See you all for grape picking this afternoon?"

They all nodded, while I remained classily neutral.

"We'll meet out front," he said before leaving.

His jeans and T-shirt combo were identical to yesterday's outfit. Meanwhile, Quirky Sue had changed into a tie-dye dress. How had this group been friends for so long? They were so different.

I sighed. Work clothes. I didn't bring work clothes. At best I had an expensive pair of jeans and a V-neck tee. I'd already lost one outfit on this trip, I'd better not wreck a second one grape picking. When I'd packed for the trip, I'd pictured *leisurely man of the world*. The reality was dusty wineries and field labor.

Since Juniper had gotten dressed after our walk, I'd become the least-dressed person in the group for the second day in a row. After excusing myself, I went up to our rooms. I dressed quickly and fixed my hair. I decided the shoes I'd worn for the drive were best for a day traipsing through fields and wineries.

Leaving my bedroom, I was surprised to find Brittany waiting on the sectional in the main room. How long had she been there?

Patting the seat next to her, Britt said, "I'm ready to talk if you are."

"How mad are you?" I asked, sitting down.

There's probably a better, smoother way of starting mature relationship conversations, but how would I know? My only other real girlfriend was from college.

"I'm not mad" is what Brittany said, but that little scar by her right eyebrow was visible, so she clearly wasn't happy.

"So…" I paused, wondering if I should keep my mouth shut before deciding to just push through. "You haven't been avoiding me?"

Britt's eyes widened. "Was this really a conversation you were up to having last night?"

I shrugged. "Not really." Then, seeing the mug of tea I'd made Britt still untouched on the table, I asked, "And this morning?"

Heat rose up Brittany's cheeks. "Okay, so there's a chance I am…or was a little…upset."

"I knew it!" I said, pointing a finger in her face. A moment later I remembered I wasn't a third grader, but it was hard to recapture an air of maturity.

For Britt's part, her mouth trembled like she was trying really hard to remain serious.

"Sorry." I raised my hands. "So, dear girlfriend, me not recognizing Tasha upset you. Is this a matter you wish to discuss further?"

Brittany raised an eyebrow. "Where'd you learn to talk like that?"

Squaring my shoulders, I tried to look offended. "I always talk like this. It's not like my work has mandatory communication seminars."

"Clearly." Britt's voice was dry.

Neither of us said anything more, and I began fighting the temptation to check the time. If Tasha had been killed because of something in the winery, I wanted to find out what. The tour was getting added on to Hannah's day, and I didn't want to miss her free time. But I couldn't check the clock. Brittany needed to know she was my priority.

Should I ask her to Christmas?

Yeah, no. Definitely not. We needed to be on firmer ground before I brought up something major.

Britt shifted on the couch, her hands fluttering before tucking invisible strands of hair behind her ears. "It's irrational," she said. "But finding out you didn't recognize your ex when she was dying in your arms...well, it made me wonder if you'd remember me in a few years."

I let out a sigh. How was I supposed to answer that? Also (and this was probably the wrong thing to focus on), I had to set the record straight. "Okay, so for starters, I didn't forget Tasha." I sounded impatient, so I tried again. "Look at the photos; she was way different."

Wait...I'd be in the photos...

"Actually, don't bother with the photos. But trust me. It's quite the transformation. And yes, if we break up and a decade later I run into you and you've dyed your hair pink, are wearing large glasses, and are dressed like a pop star, I might not recognize you. But there's no way I'd ever forget you."

A faint smile played on Brittany's lips. Then she asked, "Even if you got dementia?"

I frowned, before coming up with an answer I was super proud of. And it was all thanks to Juniper making me watch a Ryan Gosling movie.

"If I got dementia, I'd expect you to visit every day"—I laced her fingers between mine—"and tell me the story of how we met."

Brittany's lips trembled, but she managed not to laugh. "Holt, you're quoting *The Notebook*."

"What notebook?"

CHAPTER 5

J uniper was waiting on the front porch when Britt and I stepped outside. She smirked at the sight of us, somehow knowing we'd made up. I tried not to be bothered, yet little sisters can be so annoying.

"Hannah told me to head over as soon as we're ready," Juniper said.

"Are Paul and Sienna coming?" I asked.

"They have plans," Brittany said.

"Like an actual date," Juniper said.

I nodded.

That wasn't a good enough response for Juniper. "Hot-air balloon, Holt. Paul's taking his girlfriend on a hot-air balloon ride."

"That's nice," I said, thankful I was wearing my sunglasses so they could hide my annoyance.

Juniper waited for Britt to leave the porch before she grabbed my arm and whispered, "Paul is wayyy more romantic than you."

Who cared that Paul was taking Sienna on a hot-air balloon ride? I was taking Brittany to the crime scene of my murdered ex...Sure it might not look as fun on social media, but the tour should be educational.

"Did you hear me?" Juniper asked.

Instead of responding to my lack of romance, I asked, "Where's your husband?"

Juniper's eyes flicked away for a second before meeting mine. "He's on a business trip."

I gave a mock frown. "And what's his business?"

"That's none of your business."

If anything, Juniper was being more cryptic about his job than the last time I asked.

Hint: Jude works for the government, and my money's on spy.

We began walking to the winery and were met by Hot Hannah from an adjoining path. She was again dressed in a way that made her look effortlessly stylish. Her smile seemed natural as she greeted us, though I caught a slight tremor in her hands. "As I told Juniper, certain parts of the winery are taped off due to yesterday's...accident."

My body stiffened, and I stopped walking. While I haven't memorized the dictionary definition of *accident*, I'm pretty sure a corkscrew to the heart doesn't qualify.

Juniper was easily chatting with Hannah, so she didn't notice the comment's effect. But Britt noticed and moved back to take my arm.

Right. Time to remember I was on an undercover mission and to ignore any stupid comments about Tasha's death—even if Hannah suggested Tasha slipped on a banana peel and landed heart first on a corkscrew.

"Ready?" Britt asked.

I forced a smile. "Ready."

Hannah brought us to a side door. "This will be a lot of fun," she promised. "Just a reminder there's sensitive equipment inside. Don't touch the machinery, and never come here without a chaperone."

She waited for us all to agree before she opened the winery door and led us inside.

The interior looked unsurprisingly like a winery. Mysterious machines were set up against one wall, while the space was predominantly rows of large metal vats filled with fermenting grapes.

At first I thought the room was nicely dim; then I realized I was wearing my sunglasses. It would have been great if I could wear them for this mission. They're convenient for masking emotions. Unfortunately, sunglasses indoors is kind of taboo, and Hot Hannah might find it suspicious.

Hot Hannah was explaining the processes involved in making different types of wine. She went on and on about grape quality and the type of vats required. It was very dull. Even on a sleuthing mission, I had to hide a yawn.

When I'd known Tasha, she'd been getting a degree in psychology. What could she have uncovered at a winery that would lead to her death? And how would I find it?

We were continually steered clear of any sections near the yellow crime scene tape. But from what I could see, the tape didn't go very far into the building from the massive garage doors that Tasha had stumbled out of.

Throughout the building were little electronic boxes with green lights. One light changed to yellow as I passed, emitting a low beep. Surprised, I stepped back, tripping into Brittany.

"You okay back there?" Juniper asked, though she didn't sound very concerned.

"We're fine," I grumbled.

"Sorry," Hannah said. "I should have warned you about the air-filtration sensors."

Juniper and I shared a look, wordlessly asking if the other one knew what Hot Hannah was talking about. It was Brittany who was adult enough to ask, "What are the sensors for?"

"When grapes ferment, they produce carbon dioxide," Hannah explained, her hands moving excitedly. "The boxes monitor the air and let our HVAC system know how much additional oxygen is needed."

"Truly fascinating stuff," Juniper said, managing to sound serious. No surprise she'd be the teacher's pet.

I raised an eyebrow at Juniper, but Hot Hannah caught the motion, so I turned my face into a contemplative gaze. "This is an amazing setup. And to be able to work with your best friends must be..." I almost said *a nightmare* but stopped myself. "Must be great."

Hannah's eyes softened, and she cleared her throat. "Thank you. It was."

Was.

The word hung in the air. The three of us all caught it, but Brittany and I remained silent since Juniper had the strongest powers of persuasion.

My sister batted her innocent doe eyes. "*Was?* Surely the winery will be all right."

Hannah wiped under her eyes. I hadn't noticed any tears, but her hands were definitely shaking.

"The winery was Rose's," she said, like it was some big secret that I hadn't already figured out. "She'd been sick for a while and told us her affairs were all in order. We thought...or, I thought that meant..." Hannah shook her head. "But she left it all to her daughter. A child she'd never seen after giving the baby up for adoption."

Whoa.

It suddenly made sense. Tasha had been adopted.

"That woman." Hannah gestured in the direction of the crime scene tape. "She was the new owner."

Juniper's eyes had turned wide with surprise. "But I thought you didn't know Natasha?"

Hannah shook her head. "I didn't. They said Rose left the vineyard to her daughter, but I didn't know it was that woman until this morning. Brad called Rose's lawyer as soon as we found out."

A headache began forming between my temples. Presumably from all the carbon dioxide I was inhaling.

"Poor Tasha," Juniper said more to herself than anyone else.

It was the wrong thing to say. Hot Hannah's face turned cold as she fixed her perfect blouse. "Really? Who was Natasha to Rose? The heart disease must have affected her mind. She wasn't getting enough blood to her brain."

Did that happen with heart disease? I glanced at Britt, but she was giving Hot Hannah her full attention.

"Her friends have been with her for decades. And Natasha? It's not like they ever had a relationship. The baby was adopted as soon as she was born."

"Of course," Brittany said in her placating paramedic voice.

Hold on. Was Britt worried Hot Hannah would have a breakdown? I examined Hannah, but I wasn't sure what to look for.

My hand rested on a guardrail by a set of stairs leading up to the tops of a row of stainless-steel tanks. "Can we look here?" I asked, hoping a change of subject would help—plus, I wanted a higher view of the winery.

"Not those!" Hannah's words were so harsh, my hand flew off the railing like I'd been electrocuted.

Hannah tried to recover with a light laugh. "Sorry. Those tanks are for Rose's Rosé. It's our bestseller, and we're a little paranoid about losing our trade secrets."

I nodded. "Of course."

"Here." Hannah led us to another set of metal stairs. "Let me show you the fermenting Pinot."

Once we were up the stairs, we got an overhead view of the vats. These tanks didn't have lids on them and were full of pulpy liquid that wasn't the right color for wine.

"...Pinots have open tanks," Hannah was explaining as she led us along the open containers filled with almost-magenta liquid, clumpy with all the mashed grapes.

"Why does it look funny?" Juniper asked.

Had my sister really just called fancy wine *funny*?

"That's one of the colors it turns during the fermentation process," Hannah said.

"Have you ever considered bottling it while it's magenta?" I asked.

Hot Hannah's nose came up. "No. The taste would be all wrong."

What was I thinking trying to joke around with Hot Hannah? If the woman found anything humorous, it would probably be some centuries-old poet that I'd never heard of.

Juniper leaned over the railing to get a better look.

"Don't inhale," Hannah warned. "Breathing in the fumes makes people dizzy."

Juniper stepped away from the railing, and we walked along the row.

"Now, over there"—Hannah pointed to a door in the back wall—"is where we store the bottled wine and experiment with new..." But my attention wasn't on their storage room. Instead, I was looking at the row of rosé tanks. They seemed identical to all the other tanks. What had spooked Hot Hannah?

From this vantage, I could see where the crime scene tape ended in the winery. It didn't exactly lead to the row of rosé, but that could have been an oversight. How exactly did the police decide what to section off?

"Holt?" Britt said.

"Hm?"

"Hannah wanted to know if you had any questions."

Since I didn't think she'd appreciate me asking *What's the secret to your rosé?* I shook my head.

Juniper and Britt said the expected pleasantries, while I gave a nod and said, "Thanks."

Hannah led us back outside before locking the door behind us.

Britt took my arm again, and not wanting to be left out, Juniper repeated the gesture on my other side. We walked in silence, unable to say anything with Hannah still in earshot.

She'd given away a lot. But it only made the list of questions grow. Why had Rose left Tasha the vineyard? Had Rose really died of natural causes? Was Tasha killed because she was the heiress, or had she been murdered for something she'd discovered about the winery?

We'd just gotten far enough away from Hannah that I was about to start talking, when Quirky Sue popped up with a tray of quiche.

"I'm so glad I ran into you," Quirky Sue said. "The terrace is all set up, and your friends just returned."

Was this our lunch? It was still morning. I glanced at Juniper. Did she know about this ambush meal? But Juniper's expression gave nothing away.

While it was too early for a regular lunch, the terrace was set up with an array of finger foods. There were no other guests, so it seemed a little extreme for just the five of us. And with Brad, Hannah, and Sue hovering in the background, I couldn't relax. Also, I was underdressed in my jeans and V-neck and contemplated sneaking away to toss on a button-up over my shirt.

"Would you stop fidgeting?" Juniper whispered. "You're dressed like everyone else."

Did Juniper think she was helping?

This was a less formal tasting than the day before. There was an assortment of bottles and goblets lined up next to the food, and we were supposed to help ourselves. Juniper started the festivities by being the first person to pour herself a glass.

"How was the hot-air balloon?" Brittany asked when we reached Paul and Sienna.

As if on cue, Sienna leaned into Paul, and he wrapped his arm around her.

"Very...memorable," Paul said.

"That's a glowing recommendation," I said. "Britt, maybe we should go."

Sienna pursed her lips. "It wasn't bad; it was just..."

"Loud," Paul finished. "And kind of..."

"Lurchy," Sienna added.

I may have been smirking. Still, that wasn't a good reason for Juniper to elbow me in the stomach.

"Be nice. Look at how hard Paul and Sienna are trying to be romantic. Do you ever try to be romantic?"

It was on the tip of my tongue to tell Juniper it was none of her business, but Brittany had an answer before me—is my girlfriend a rock star, or what?

"Trust me. Holt's plenty romantic."

My shoulders expanded, though I shouldn't act smug around my sister.

Juniper remained unconvinced. "Mm-hmm." She popped her hip. "Paul took Sienna up in a hot-air balloon. What's Holt done?"

Okay. Here was a perfect example of why your girlfriend should never meet your family. Christmas together was a bad idea.

When she didn't get an immediate reply, Juniper continued. "Last night Sienna told me when Paul was in jail, he tried to break up with her so she could date other people. But Sienna kept visiting. Once he realized she wouldn't stop, Paul started saying at the end of each visit, *We're still broken up, but I love you.* Has Holt ever done anything like that?"

My jaw ticked. Juniper'd had a front-row seat a couple of months ago to just how far I was willing to go for Brittany. When I glanced at Britt, she gave a slight shake of her head. So instead of giving a serious answer, I took a deep breath and asked, "Does thinking your girlfriend was a murderer count as romantic?"

Britt's mouth quirked.

I'd done good.

"Nope. Not romantic," Juniper said.

Britt's eyes twinkled. "How about throwing up multiple times on the first date?"

Juniper wrinkled her nose. "Absolutely not."

"Hm." I wrapped an arm around Britt. "I guess I'm not romantic."

Brittany pressed a kiss on my cheek. "I guess not."

I grinned. Not being romantic had its perks. For a moment I forgot everything but Britt's brown eyes gazing up at me. When I was able to look away, my eyes landed right on Juniper. She was making a face I didn't recognize. "You're right, sis," I said. "Is that what you wanted to hear?"

I don't know what my sister's response was, because Britt had pulled my head down to hers, and we were kissing. I'd never been so glad I wasn't romantic. I owed Juniper a thank-you.

Paul cleared his throat, and I got the impression he'd argue I was too romantic. He was holding two goblets of wine, one clearly intended for Sienna, but instead, he asked, "Holt, have you tried the rosé?"

I arched an eyebrow. "I don't think so."

"Here." Paul shoved a glass in my hands, but his eyes were on Brittany.

This was proving to be quite the awkward affair. Taking a step away from Britt, I swirled the wine before taking a sip.

I'm not a *wine drinker*. Still, I know enough. And it's a good thing we were on the patio, because I spat the liquid the moment it touched my tongue. There was no way I was swallowing that.

I shot Paul a dirty look. What had he done?

"Holt!" Juniper called.

"What? It tasted like stale vinegar."

Juniper pressed her lips together, her fun influencer persona completely gone. "It's good to experience new things, not spit at fancy events."

"Fancy? I'm wearing jeans, Juniper. Jeans."

Behind us, Brittany was whispering to Paul, who was shaking his head.

Slowly, he brought the glass to his nose and sniffed. We all watched as he took a sip. While Paul actually swallowed, it was with a grimace. "That's not anything I'd call wine."

Juniper looked between us like she thought we were in cahoots. "You're both wrong." After taking my goblet, she took a mouthful—before becoming the second person to spew wine at a fancy event.

"Very classy, sis," I said, applauding.

While the managers didn't care when I'd rejected their wine, Hannah, Brad, and Sue came running after Juniper's spit take.

"What happened?" Bad Brad asked, getting a little too close to Juniper until Hot Hannah caught his eye.

Juniper had recovered quickly and gave a radiant smile. "Oh, nothing. We got a bottle that was open too long."

Hannah looked from her husband to Quirky Sue. "They should all be fresh bottles."

Bad Brad strode to the wine table. "Which bottle?"

"The rosé," Paul answered.

More lines than I thought possible appeared on Brad's face. "It's last year's vintage." His eyes darkened, and he seemed to be using all his energy to *not* look in Quirky Sue's direction.

Quirky Sue covered her mouth, shaking her head. "I don't know how that happened."

"You had all morning to prepare." Hannah's voice held barely controlled anger.

"That's what I did!" Sue said. Her eyes began to water. "As soon as breakfast was over, I worked on this."

"Then why—" Hannah started to ask, but Brad interrupted.

"No matter," he said. Then he stormed off with the offending bottle of wine.

Quirky Sue followed moments later with mine and Paul's goblets of rosé.

Hannah stared after them. Then she closed her eyes and took a deep breath. When she opened them, she had transformed from mad friend to charming hostess. She began talking about her favorite wines while giving us all healthy pours.

As I sipped, I tried to figure out what was wrong with the rosé. First with the winery vats and then with the bottles. The problem was, an unscripted Hannah was very good at her job, and with Juniper's help, the event turned into quite the party. Plenty of wines were more than sampled, and Sue's finger foods were delicious.

The sun was high in the blue sky, heating the world to a comfortable napping temperature. I yawned. A combination of the wine and an early morning had me sleepy. I was making plans to sneak away and stretch out in the sun on an abandoned lawn chair. The only holdup was deciding whether I should invite Britt.

I was way more likely to take naps than Britt—both intentional and accidental—but would she nap on vacation?

Deciding it was best to ask, I'd just gotten to her side when Average Joe showed up, his clothes damper and dirtier than when we'd seen him at breakfast. "You ready to go?"

What? Now? They'd stuffed us full of wine and expected us to walk a straight line with blades in our hands?

"We'll be ready as soon as I have Chouzie," Juniper said.

Brittany laced her fingers between mine like she was afraid I'd bolt. "Relax," she said. "It'll be fun."

I raised an eyebrow.

Britt giggled. "It'll be fun for the rest of us."

Sure it would.

I didn't fight as she walked us to Joe's truck, but I balked at getting in the pickup bed. Were we expected to jostle around an open truck bed while Average Joe went off-roading between grapevines?

Sensing my unease, Britt suggested I ride in the cab with Joe.

Keep in mind, I'm a confident adult who would never fall victim to peer pressure, but Sienna and Paul were already in the back of the truck, talking and laughing like it was no big thing. The only reason Juniper wasn't right beside them was because she was inside getting Chouzie.

"Holt," Brittany said quietly. "It's fine. Don't worry about them."

My jaw twitched. It wasn't just that Juniper would make fun of me if I rode in the front, but I'd also be ditching Brittany for a safer seat.

Squaring my shoulders, I climbed in. If the truck hit a massive pothole and tipped over, I'd be right beside Britt. I offered her my hand. The scar by Britt's eyebrow was outlined, but she made no further comment. There wasn't ideal seating. More like shoving random supplies around and claiming a spot.

Uncomfortable or not, I was still nicely warmed by the sun and found keeping my eyes open to be increasingly difficult.

Juniper better hurry up. I couldn't fall asleep. Not only had I experienced a recent string of bad luck sleeping in vehicles, but if I wasn't careful, I'd get tetanus. Still, I was in trouble. My eyes were half-closed and I was struggling not to yawn when I overheard Sienna asking Paul, "Didn't you see her?"

The question itself was vague, but the way she'd almost whispered it and glanced to the truck's cab, where Joe sat, turned on my sleuthing senses.

Paul shrugged. "I don't know. Maybe."

"Does this have something to do with Tasha?" I asked—since apparently wine makes me chatty.

"Well..." Sienna leaned toward me and lowered her voice so I could barely hear. "Sue said she'd spent all morning getting ready for our patio tasting, but I saw her in the vineyard when we were in the hot-air balloon."

"Don't hot-air balloons get pretty high in the sky?" Brittany asked. "How well did you see this person?"

Sienna shook her head. "The person I saw was wearing a tie-dye dress and was the general weight and build of Sue."

"That should hold up in court," I said—momentarily forgetting I wasn't with my lawyer buddy.

"But Paul didn't see her?" Brittany asked.

Paul winked. "I only had eyes for Sienna."

"That's way too cheesy," I groaned as Britt and Sienna tried not to smile.

Paul shrugged. "What? I love my girlfriend. Besides, it doesn't matter whether I spotted Sue in the vineyard. If Sienna saw her, she was there."

"Right, sorry," Brittany said.

Sue was in the vineyard? Why would she lie about that?

"Do you think Sue was lying to us or to the other managers?" I asked.

Paul frowned. "What's the difference?"

Both Britt and Sienna were also watching me like they didn't know the answer. "Well"—I smoothed back a lock of hair that had flopped onto my forehead—"Sue told everyone she'd spent all morning getting ready after Brad and Hannah were mad about her setting out the wrong bottle of wine."

"Uh-huh," Britt said. "So she could have gone for a walk and lost track of time but didn't want her friends accusing her of being lazy or bad at her job."

"I don't know..." Sienna bit her lip.

"Do we have other ideas for why Sue could be lying?" Paul asked.

That was a good question. And no one answered right away as we tried to think of suspicious reasons for Sue to lie about being in the vineyard. But I came up empty. The vineyard would be a good place to hide something like the murder weapon, but the corkscrew had been left with Tasha, and what else would Sue need to hide?

"We don't need to figure it out right now," Britt finally said.

My shoulders relaxed. I was so glad Brittany had let us off the hook.

Just then there was a low bark. Juniper was walking up with Chouzie. She handed me the chow chow before climbing in and closing the tailgate.

Paul tapped on the glass, and Average Joe began driving through the grapevines at a sedate pace.

Juniper had found a seat next to me and probably expected me to return the dog. But I didn't mind Chouzie's company and enjoyed the way his reddish mane ruffled in the wind.

Since she was dogless, Juniper began filming, explaining where she was going and showing how much Chouzie was enjoying the travel—thankfully keeping my face out of the video. Once she'd finished recording, Juniper moved even closer to me and asked, "Do you think Joe can hear us?"

After checking the front of the truck with its unrolled windows, I shrugged. "Unlikely."

"Great," Juniper said. "Did your girlfriend ever mention her birth dad?"

"Ex-girlfriend," I corrected.

Juniper rolled her eyes. "Whatever. You know who I meant."

Before I could answer, Brittany was leaning in to join the conversation. "I've also been wondering about the birth dad."

I sighed. This was feeling more and more like gossip than a search for justice.

"The father has to be Brad or Joe." Juniper's voice was full of excitement. "Why else would Rose give up the child if it wasn't some deep dark secret?"

I shook my head. "Okay, there are many reasons why someone might decide to—"

"My money's on Brad," Brittany interrupted.

Groaning, I muttered something about Juniper being a bad influence.

"Ugh." Juniper wrinkled her nose. "Brad's so creepy. Can you believe he's been married for decades?"

"Poor Hannah," Britt said.

Rose and Brad? The woman from the photos looked proud and confident. Not the sort of person to be fooled by Brad's charms.

"We don't know anything about Rose," I said. "What makes you think she'd even be interested in Brad? He's so..." There wasn't an adequate word to finish that sentence with.

"Holt, you're as bad as we are," Brittany said, resting her head on my shoulder.

I felt Paul's eyes on me, but I wasn't going to apologize for his sister liking me.

"Okay, okay," Juniper said. "But if Tasha's dad was one of Rose's friends and it wasn't Brad, that would leave—"

The slam of the truck door alerted the three of us we'd stopped moving. Average Joe lowered the truck bed's gate. "Time to get to work," he said.

We stared at him wide-eyed. Was he Tasha's father?

CHAPTER 6

Grape picking went about how you'd expect. Paul, the professional fisherman, took to it with almost robotic precision. Juniper giggled as Chouzie tried to lead her in circles, and most of the party had a lot of fun thanks to the wine at lunch.

I didn't love it. And it wasn't going to make me like wine more. If anything, discovering all the dirt and bugs involved was going to make me like wine less.

The sun was a little too bright even with sunglasses, but I trudged down the rows doing my due diligence. I'd wanted to talk with Average Joe. I needed a way to bring up Rose and Tasha. But right after our brief training where he gave us all hooks to harvest grapes with, he got called away to a different section of land.

He wasn't gone five minutes before I felt stranded and was searching for his truck's return. Not for Tasha's sake but for the selfish reason that I wanted to stop laboring in the sun. Seriously, how long were we expected to work out here? And at my naptime.

"Arrrrgh!" Juniper said, holding the blade like she was Captain Hook with a grinning chow chow sidekick.

I ignored her and continued harvesting. The only thing I knew for sure was it was Juniper's fault we were stuck in the fields. And if there was a quota we had to meet before Average Joe brought us back, I wanted us to reach it as soon as possible.

When Juniper understood she wasn't getting a new pirate friend, she lowered the hook. "What's been your favorite wine?" she asked.

I kept ignoring her and continued working steadily at cutting down clumps of grapes. I didn't have Paul's dexterity, but I was working at a decent pace.

"Who do you think killed Tasha?" she tried.

In the past, Juniper had been the John Watson to my Sherlock Holmes, but I wasn't about to let her off so easily and continued working without so much as a glance her way.

"It sure is lucky we were able to come this season," Juniper said. She moved to the other side of me and fingered a bunch of grapes I was about to cut. "It's perfect timing to experience the harvest."

I glared at Juniper, and she giggled.

"Come on," she said. "There's no need to be so serious."

Stretching my arms and back, I said, "I'm the only one who's working. I have every right to be serious."

Juniper shook her head like I was being a pill. Then she bit her lip. "Actually, I was wondering if you could..."

I raised an eyebrow. Juniper was in no position to be asking for favors.

She looked to the sky before finally saying, "I'd like you to film me."

Oh. Weird. Not what I expected.

"Normally Jude films when we're on trips, but he had this work thing, and it's not easy to hold a phone and cut grapes at the same time."

"Fine," I said just as Juniper was opening her mouth to say more.

She nodded and, clearly worried I'd change my mind, handed me her phone and got to work.

There's a slight chance I *forgot* to hit record the first time and let Juniper monologue while she worked for a while before I caught my mistake...What can I say? These things happen.

When Juniper wrapped up her streaming, I'd assumed she'd wander away with Chouzie. Instead, she stayed and continued casually grape picking around me.

"Have you talked to Britt?" Juniper asked as we worked.

I shrugged, not sure what she was referencing.

"About Christmas. Who knows when Mom and Dad will be back in the States, and I don't see you flying to Australia anytime soon."

Me, go to Australia? Definitely not. I'd studied abroad in Germany for a semester, and while I don't regret doing it, the experience showed just how bad I am with drastic time changes and jet lag.

"Did you ask?" Juniper asked.

"I haven't talked to Britt about my Christmas plans."

"Will you?"

I frowned. Britt's Mom didn't like me. And that was before her only daughter moved from Oregon to Washington to be near me. How would Mrs. Asato react if I stole Britt for Christmas?

"Hey." Juniper moved to stand toe to toe with me and stared straight up at my sunglasses. "It doesn't hurt to ask. You've met her family. This would give her a chance to get to know yours. Besides," Juniper said, beginning to walk away, "Casey will bring Harper and Baxter. You'll get to see how much Britt likes kids."

Kids?

Before I got a chance to process Juniper's *kids* comment, she stirred the pot even more. "Did you and Tasha ever talk about kids?"

Tasha? Kids?

"No! We weren't *that* serious."

Juniper huffed out a breath. "I meant because she was a social worker at a children's hospital."

Oh. My bad.

Juniper began tapping on her phone. "According to her Instagram, she's been there for the last three years."

Hadn't she wanted to be a psychologist?

I shook my head. "I can't remember her saying anything about kids or becoming a social worker." While it was never a job she'd talked about, it was easy to imagine her being great at it.

Tasha's death was bringing up long-forgotten memories. She was one of the few people who made sure I had fun. Once she'd convinced me we should sing an Elton John duet. We were decent...until we reached the harmony, and it sounded so bad she'd collapsed laughing onstage.

Tasha had dumped me because I was too closed off. Had she found someone else who was better for her? Did she enjoy working at the children's hospital?

"Holt?"

My voice sort of cracked when I asked, "Was she happy?"

I don't know why I asked that. It's not like it mattered now. Still, with Juniper living on social media, she'd be able to tell if the fun and happy photos on Tasha's profile were fake or genuine.

Juniper's eyes softened. She was probably internally high-fiving herself for getting me to express an emotion. "Here." She gave me her phone with Tasha's Instagram profile open. "See for yourself."

"Thanks."

Chouzie began pulling at his leash. He was ready to move on, yet Juniper hesitated. "But yes, Tasha was happy."

A tightness in my chest released.

"Okay."

I didn't say anything more, and Juniper knew me well enough to leave.

I checked to make sure Brittany wasn't nearby before I scrolled through Tasha's photos. Should I feel guilty for looking at snapshots of my ex's life? What would Brittany think?

———◈———

I was quiet on the bumpy ride back. Britt probably figured I was tired and grumpy. She spent the ride chatting with Sienna, her fingers laced casually in mine. I rested my eyes on the drive but not because I was about to fall asleep. More because I was processing the snapshots I'd seen of Tasha's life. Plus, I couldn't get Christmas out of my mind.

Why would Juniper mention kids?

Of course I love kids. What kind of monster doesn't like kids? Still, I prefer life without all the yells, crying, and spills that come with children. I barely tolerated kids when I was a kid. Now I'm a crotchety old man stuck in my ways.

Did I want kids? Up until a few months ago I didn't want a serious girlfriend. Now look at me.

When the truck stopped by Rose's Repose, I slipped away from the group. I needed to clear my head, and I wouldn't be able to do that surrounded by people.

I wandered along gravel walkways. There were tons of interconnecting footpaths all with a variety of plants. Sue probably took care of them now, but had they once been Rose's? Tasha's dorm room had been filled with potted plants. Were green thumbs genetic?

I should find Quirky Sue and find out why she'd lied about her morning in the vineyard. But that needed to wait until I was no longer about to drop into the fetal position from being around people too long.

There was also the Christmas problem. Mom would want a head count before she rented a house. If I did invite Britt to Christmas, the sooner the better. But we hadn't been together very long. Was it too soon to invite her on a trip that was months away?

Juniper appeared without Chouzie from an intersecting path and gave a wave when she saw me. "I thought I'd better check and make sure I hadn't freaked you out too badly."

"I'm fine." I continued walking, hoping Juniper would take the hint and leave me alone.

She didn't. But at least she stayed silent, only shooting me worried glances from time to time.

"Hey," she said, gesturing to where Average Joe stood near the crime scene tape at the winery. "Let's go ask him what he knew about Tasha."

Juniper set off without checking to see if I'd follow. Of course I followed. Not only was I curious, but one of these days Juniper's big mouth would get her into trouble and she'd need backup.

Joe had moved on from the crime scene tape and had disappeared into the winery through a side door opposite the one Hannah had used for our tour. Juniper didn't hesitate at the entrance but pulled the door open and walked in like she owned the place. The room was dim. Only light from a few high windows and the rare emergency light brightened the space.

"Joe," Juniper called. "Is now a good time for a few questions?"

There was no answer, but in the distance there was the muffled sound of voices. We began walking in that direction. Then there was a sudden yell, followed by a splash and the pound of running footsteps.

For a moment I froze as my brain processed the sounds. Either Average Joe had pushed someone or been pushed into a vat of fermenting grapes radiating carbon dioxide fumes.

Here was a surprisingly easy way to unmask Tasha's killer. All I had to do was chase the pusher. But if I did that there'd be another dead body, and I couldn't let that happen.

So I bolted to the wine vats. Juniper had read my mind and was right behind me.

I sprinted up one flight of stairs, and Juniper chose the row next to mine so we had a better chance of finding the vat with our victim. I pulled out my phone and called Brittany as I ran.

"Hello?"

"Get to the winery," I shouted and hung up without giving any other explanation. Britt's trained for emergencies. She'd know what to do.

I was halfway through my row of vats when I saw him. Average Joe was floating face down in the pool of wine.

"Here," I yelled, before slipping off my shoes and tossing my sunglasses, phone, and wallet onto the walkway.

"Holt, don't!" Juniper shrieked from her row. I ignored her, took a deep breath, and lowered myself into a pool of wine.

Back in my lifeguarding days, I could hold my breath for over ninety seconds. How long could I last years later swimming through grape pulp? Any breath I took would just fill my body with carbon dioxide—which is not what you want.

I paddled over to Joe easily enough. In a good news, bad news sort of deal, he didn't thrash or flail when I got to him. It made moving him easier, but he was giving no signs of life.

I'd managed to keep my head from dunking down into the wine. Still, my eyes were stinging from the gas, and my lungs were throbbing without oxygen.

Juniper was waiting at the rim, saying things I didn't bother paying attention to. When I reached the side, Juniper bent over and grabbed one of Joe's arms. She began tugging while I tried to lift. After a few seconds of this, my lungs gave out, and I took an involuntary breath.

My lungs began stinging for a new reason, and my grip on Joe loosened. Large hands appeared and began dragging Joe out of the vat. My body was truly panicking, and I took a second desperate breath. One of Joe's legs collided with my head, dunking me under the red liquid.

I think I got my head above the surface, but everything was so muddled. I couldn't breathe, could barely see, and there were voices, but I couldn't understand them. I'd been treading water, but it was getting difficult to keep my body upright. I was slowing down, about to take a third breath, when Britt's voice cut through all the confusion. "Holt Jacobs, give me your hand." I reached up blindly and mumbled a protest when rough hands grabbed me and I was lifted painfully up and over the tank.

Once I was safely on the walkway, the hands let go, and I lay there. I was coughing and spluttering, taking deep breaths but never getting quite enough air.

Then it happened. Water was poured on my face.

"Juniper," I croaked, without knowing for sure it was her.

At some point I rolled over from my back to my hands and knees, coughing and panting like a mad dog.

"Holt, how are you doing?" It was Brittany's voice, calm and steady.

"Great. I'm great," I gasped, before my arms gave out and I fell onto my stomach.

"Take him outside. Let him get some fresh air." It was Brittany again.

Strange. She was acting unusually bossy.

I yelped when hands dug into my armpits and I was hoisted unceremoniously to my feet.

"It's okay. It's okay," Juniper kept saying beside me.

"Help us out here," grunted a voice I didn't recognize. Lolling my head to one side, I found Brad was there, his face taut. *Brad?* Was he the one who pulled me out? Had Bad Brad saved my life?

"Britt?" I mumbled.

"She's with Joe right now," Juniper said. "Come on, one foot in front of the other."

I twisted to find Britt and nearly sent the three of us sprawling. Brad gave a yell before catching the railing. He was stronger than I expected.

Brittany was bent over Joe, who remained motionless. I know I shouldn't be jealous. But what good is having a paramedic girlfriend if, during an emergency, she spends her time with another dude?

We made it to the stairs, and for some reason I couldn't quite remember, we had to go down. Something was very wrong inside me. "I'm going to be sick," I muttered.

"Not in my winery," Brad said.

It sounded like Juniper giggled. We still hadn't taken a step down the metal stairs. As things stood, an accident seemed likely.

"Holt could go down step by step on his butt," Juniper suggested.

That wouldn't work. I would've explained why, but I was panting and could feel myself sweating through the wine.

Then Paul appeared at the bottom of the stairs. His face was set with the same professional calm as Britt.

"Is Brittany okay?" he asked.

"Yeah, she's fine." Juniper readjusted her hold on me. "Can you get Holt outside? Brittany said he needs fresh air."

Paul nodded and got me outside with relative ease. Or I assume he did. To be honest, that part's kind of hazy. I don't know if this makes sense, but it was like I had the flu on a bad allergy day.

Next thing I knew, I was lying on the grass, half propped against Juniper, with sirens wailing in the distance. "Is that for me?"

"It's for Joe."

"Juniper?"

"Yeah?"

"If you take any pictures of me, don't send them to Mom for at least a month."

Juniper started shaking with suppressed laughter. "That might be hard. You're kind of purple."

Sometime after that Brittany appeared.

"Britt?" I sat up only to start coughing. That didn't matter. She would make everything better.

Brittany crouched in front of me and stared so deeply into my eyes, she could probably see my soul—though she may have been checking my pupils.

"Are they sending a second ambulance?" Juniper asked.

"They don't have one," Britt said. "Paul's getting his Subaru. I'm not waiting for the ambulance to come back from bringing Joe."

Instead of making things better, Britt had ordered a trip to the ER. Such a hassle. Shouldn't I be consulted on whether or not I wanted to go to the hospital?

I think I groaned. Which was my only comment about being kidnapped.

Paul arrived and set up a tarp in his back seat before I was loaded in. First plastic sheets and now a plastic seat? What was my life coming to?

Brittany sat beside me, and Juniper rode up front with Paul. "How are you?" Britt asked, her scar the only thing betraying she was worried.

"Horrible," I said. "I want to lie down, and you're making me go to the hospital."

Britt's mouth twitched as she fought a smile. "I know. I'm the worst."

"You said it, not me." For a moment I wondered if that was too mean, but Britt seemed fine, so I rested my head against the massive tarp Paul was making me sit on.

It was official. I'd ruined another outfit.

The whining of the ambulance caught up to us, and Paul pulled over so it could pass. That's when I remembered to ask, "How's Joe?"

"Still alive," Brittany said, "but unconscious when the other paramedics arrived." Britt analyzed my face before adding, "He had a nasty bump to the head."

I nodded. "Yeah. It sounded like someone knocked him into the vat."

"That's what I thought too," Juniper said, twisting from her spot beside Paul. "But I didn't see anyone. Did you?"

I shook my head, and the rest of the drive went by in silence.

The hospital was a huge inconvenience. For starters, my ID and insurance card were in my wallet somewhere on the winery floor. Then they made me change into a hospital gown.

Have you ever tried to remove wine-soaked jeans while experiencing flu-like symptoms? I don't recommend it. But it's not like I was going to ask for help. The help I'd get would be some stranger with scissors cutting me out of my pants.

The jeans would probably be fine after going through the wash. But if they were cut into shreds, they'd be unwearable.

There was a swirl of doctors and nurses with questions. Tests and oxygen. I grew less loopy as the process progressed, but that only brought out the crankiness.

I was alone in a treatment room waiting to be discharged when Cop Kid showed up wanting my statement.

"Are you well enough to go over what happened?" he asked.

"No," I said.

Cop Kid sat down, ignoring my answer.

"How did you end up in the winery? Isn't it off-limits for guests without an escort?"

My eyes closed, and I rested my head against the half-upright bed. Of course this was happening.

"Mr. Jacobs?"

"Yeah, I'm here," I said, raising my head. "Sorry, I'm a little off today. I don't know if you're aware, but this is a hospital and this plastic bracelet"—I waved my wrist—"shows I'm one of the patients."

Cop Kid covered his mouth with his hand, his eyes crinkling. After a few seconds he gave a cough before returning to the interview like nothing had happened.

"So, why were you in the winery?"

I wasn't going to lie to the man, but I'd do my best to keep most of the truth to myself. Telling the police I was following Joe to ask if he was the birth father of my murdered ex-girlfriend sounded like I was auditioning for a soap opera.

"Joe had just taken us grape picking. My sister and I saw him go into the winery and followed since we had a few questions."

"I see," Cop Kid said. But there was something about his tone, how his eyes stayed slightly crinkled, that gave me the impression he knew I wasn't taking the interview seriously.

"And Joe Shaw. How did he end up in the tank?"

Had this cop already talked to Juniper? Surely she'd tell him we'd *heard* but hadn't *seen* what happened.

"There were sounds of an argument, then a splash." I shrugged. "I don't know who was with Joe."

After I answered, Cop Kid gave a slow nod like my information was super important. "And you're sure you didn't see anyone? This is the second incident you've come across at the winery in two days."

What was he implying?

I straightened, anger flaring. "I nearly died getting Joe out of the tank. I wouldn't have pushed him in."

The Cop Kid coughed quickly before moving to the window and standing there for some time. When he returned, his face had the same look of being not quite serious.

"What?" I asked.

Cop Kid tilted his head, allowing the faintest of smiles. "You remind me of my cousin."

"Um…" Was that supposed to mean something? "Thank you?"

His lips twitched, but he stayed almost serious. "Now, about Natasha. Since we're here, I have a few follow-up questions about your relationship."

"We don't have a relationship," I said.

I stared at Cop Kid, and he stared right back. I was practically daring him to correct me. While yes, we dated in college, that was ten years, five apartments, and two jobs ago. Nothing I knew about Tasha in our former lives would help with the investigation.

"All the same," Cop Kid said, "I wanted to ask—"

Britt walked into my room carrying a semi-clear garbage bag with what was probably my wine-soaked clothes. She said, "A nurse is getting a pair of disposable scrubs, since you won't be putting these back on." Seeing the cop, Britt widened her stance, and she seemed to grow a few inches. "Your interview's done. Mr. Jacobs is in no condition to answer questions right now."

Cop Kid deflated, and I smirked. Brittany having a bossy side wasn't such a bad thing.

"Of course," Cop Kid said and gave a little bow in Britt's direction. He was halfway out the door when he turned back. "Hold on," he said. "Stay here. I'll be back in a minute."

I raised an eyebrow at Britt, who shook her head and came to stand beside me. "You're all set to go. The doctor said you'll need to take it easy the next few days since you'll be kind of sluggish, but you're cleared to leave."

"All right," I said, not really processing her words. How could it be days before I felt better? A part of me expected I'd feel this way forever, while another part assumed I'd be back to normal after a good nap.

"Paul and Juniper are already in the car. All we need is your change of clothes."

"Great," I said, leaning against her.

Britt put a hand in my hair, then quickly removed it. "Don't freak out," she said. "But your hair is all sticky."

"What!" I tried to sound outraged since me acting normal was the best way to make Brittany less worried. "I'm trying out this new conditioner. It was supposed to make my hair silky smooth."

"I'd ask for a refund," Britt said.

"Yeah."

Instead of putting her hand back in my hair, Brittany's hand cupped my neck. Strange. That's what Mom did to calm me down as a kid. I let out a long-overdue sigh...Guess it still worked as an adult.

We remained like this until Cop Kid returned carrying folded clothes. "It's nothing fancy, but they're clean and dry. Should be better than disposable scrubs."

He shoved the clothes at me, and it took a few seconds for me to catch on. Wasn't I a murder suspect? Why had he gone out of his way to give me clothes?

"Don't worry about returning them. They're old," he said.

I nodded. "Um, thanks."

Cop Kid held out his hand, and we shook. "You saved a man's life today. Don't make me arrest you tomorrow."

CHAPTER 7

C op Kid was smaller than me. The shorts were tight and stopped well above my knees. As for the sweatshirt, I'm totally serious when I say it was for a high school wrestling team. There was no year printed on it, or I would have done the math to figure out how old my young friend was. Regardless, the cop was right; it was better than the disposable scrubs.

When Britt and I returned to the car, Paul eyed me, trying to figure out if I would stain his seats. I decided to sit on the tarp without comment. As long as Britt sat beside me, I had no complaints...Well, Juniper could have moved her seat forward so I had more legroom, but other than that, no complaints.

"We'll all need to change when we get back," Juniper said. "I texted Sue, and she said we can use the laundry room that's across from the kitchen. Now, is anyone besides Holt showering?"

Why were they all changing?

What with all the brain fog brought on by carbon dioxide poisoning, I was still operating a couple of steps behind. Then I noticed it. Britt's clothes were splotched red like they'd gotten a strange tie-dye, Paul's shoulder and down his side were dyed red, and when Juniper twisted back to face us, I could see she was the worst of the bunch. Her shirt was practically one big stain. Why hadn't Paul made Juniper sit on a tarp?

Juniper caught my gaze and shook her head. "Yes, you've ruined a lot of clothes today."

"I blame Joe," I said.

"Not the person who pushed him?" Juniper asked.

I shrugged. "That works too."

Back at the house, Juniper and Paul quickly disappeared upstairs. I was still weak and a little dizzy but was able to walk up the stairs. The problem was, Britt felt the need to supervise.

I was resting at the second-floor landing with sweat breaking out around my temples, when I side-eyed Britt. "You know I'll make it."

Britt nodded. "Of course you will."

"So you"—I paused to take a few deep breaths—"can go, and I'll see you in a minute."

Britt smiled, but there was hardheaded stubbornness just under the surface. "Not a chance."

When I finally made it to the room, I was tempted to collapse on the couch to recover, but I might not get up again. Juniper was right. I needed a shower. I reeked of wine, and while not exactly purple, my skin wasn't a normal color. After stopping by my room to get clean sweats, I was ready to shower. I'd made it to the bathroom door, when Britt stopped me.

"Holt, could you do me a favor?"

What could Brittany want? "Um...maybe."

"Leave the bathroom door unlocked."

I looked from Britt to the door, then back to Britt. "Excuse me?"

Britt shrugged, trying so hard to seem nonchalant. "Just this once."

My eyes squeezed shut as realization hit. "I'm not going to pass out in the shower."

"Of course not" is what she said, but from the set of her jaw, I got the impression that if I didn't go along with the unlocked door policy, her next plan involved removing the door.

I tried to run a hand through my sticky hair. I always lock the bathroom door, even when I'm alone in my apartment. This was so wrong.

The scar by Britt's eyebrow was well defined. She was worried and wanted to keep me safe.

I could do this for her. Sighing, I said, "Fine. But I'm great, and this is unnecessary." I closed the door without waiting for a reply.

I almost screamed at my reflection. The bathroom mirror didn't do me any favors. My hair was a few shades darker than normal and sticking together in weird clumps. I was wearing clothes too small for me, and I was a little more purple than I'd originally thought. With Brittany listening on the other side of the door, I swallowed a groan and got into the shower.

I didn't pass out.

There was a moment when I decided to sit down in the tub to rest a bit, but that could happen to anyone.

By the end of the shower, I'd scrubbed myself so much, I didn't know what was redness from the scrubbing versus dye from the wine. After drying off my hair, I decided not to bother with product. Lying down was becoming a necessity, and if my hair was a poofy mess after, so be it.

"Britt?" I called through the door as I pulled on my joggers.

"Yeah?"

"I'm still alive."

"I figured," Britt was saying right as I opened the door.

After giving her a quick kiss, I moved past her toward my bedroom.

"Holt," Brittany said with a little extra emotion in her voice. "Could you come to the couch?"

I scrubbed a hand over my face, reminding myself I was an adult and should use my words. "Britt, I have to lie down."

Brittany bit her lip and shifted her weight from one foot to the other. "I know, but..."

Exhausted, I leaned against the wall.

"My goodness," Juniper said, rising from one of the kitchenette chairs. Had she been there the whole time? "Holt, Brittany wants to watch you sleep."

Britt began flushing and tucking invisible strands of hair behind her ears. "Not exactly. It's just I would prefer to be able to monitor your breathing and heart rate, which would be easier if you were with me on the couch."

I held a hand out to her. "You're, like, pretty worried?"

Brittany took my hand and began walking me to the couch. "I don't know about *pretty worried*. More like *moderately concerned*."

I tried to hide how happy her *moderate concern* made me. "The hospital said I was good to go."

Brittany sat down and didn't reply until I was stretched out across the couch with my head in her lap. "First off, they said to take it easy, and second, the hospital didn't watch their boyfriend swimming in a vat of carbon dioxide."

"Britt should definitely be worried," added my ever-helpful sister. "That's the Joker's origin story."

My eyes were half-closed, and I was almost too comfortable to correct her. Almost. Clearing my throat, I said, "The Joker fell into a vat of acid, not wine."

"Nerd," Juniper said.

I'd walked right into that one.

I shivered slightly, feeling strangely cold, but I was too tired to worry about a blanket and was almost asleep when an odd scraping had me cracking an eye open. Juniper stood above me. "What are you doing?" I asked, half sitting up.

My sister rolled her eyes. "Would you relax? I'm being nice."

I watched skeptically as Juniper removed the top from the ottoman, then took out a blue quilt and spread it over me.

Finally, Britt eased my head back onto her lap, before finding my hand and giving it a squeeze. "Relax," she whispered.

Muttering something unintelligible, I did as requested.

——◆◇◆——

Voices gradually entered my sleep. Brittany and Juniper were talking, but I couldn't tell what they were saying. I shifted slightly, drifting deeper when a knock had me sitting up and rubbing a hand over my face.

My sister was by the door with Quirky Sue. "Sorry for just barging in like this," Quirky Sue was saying, carrying two stacked totes. She caught sight of me. "Oh my. Did I wake you? I'm so sorry. Paul told us the three of you wouldn't be down for supper, so I brought some up." Quirky Sue set the totes on the kitchenette's small table. "There's food in the top one, and I added a bottle of Pinot."

I'm not proud of this, but I dry heaved at the mention of wine.

"Oh, uh...Then again, you've probably been around enough wine. The other tub has all your clean clothes, plus Holt's shoes and sunglasses that he left in the winery. And here"—she reached into her pocket—"are his phone and wallet."

Would she ever stop talking?

"I heard all about your heroics," Sue said, moving to stand in front of me on the couch.

Now she was talking to me. Yikes. Was it too late to pretend I was still asleep?

Quirky Sue said, "I don't know if they give out medals for that sort of thing, but you deserve one. Jumping in like that, you saved his life. We almost had two murders in two days." Quirky Sue looked at me expectantly, and I realized it was finally my turn to say something.

"Uhh." I tried to blink away the grogginess. "I'm sorry, is there any coffee?"

She laughed and looked at Brittany. "You must have your hands full with this one." Without waiting for an answer, Sue was talking about how she'd better be going and didn't want to be in the way.

At least she let herself out.

The door had just clicked shut when I remembered Quirky Sue had lied about being in the vineyard.

I struggled, trying to stand up. Somehow I was all tangled in the quilt. Before I could figure it out, Britt had rested a firm hand on my arm. "What do you need?"

"Sue lied." I was a little breathless. "I want to know why."

Brittany looked to Juniper.

My sister tossed back her hair. "I'm on it." The next second Juniper was out the door and calling down the stairs. "Sue, could you come back for a second? There's something we wanted to ask you."

Quirky Sue reentered the room, looking at us curiously. "What did you need?"

Britt and Juniper looked at me, trying to figure out whether I planned on doing the interrogating.

I was still half-asleep and my lungs were burning, but I'd at least make an attempt to question Quirky Sue. "At the tasting," I said, doing my best to make my voice sound normal, "you said you'd spent all morning getting the patio ready, but Sienna saw you walking through the vineyard."

"Oh." Color rushed to Quirky Sue's face.

Was she about to start crying? I really couldn't deal with that right now.

"How did she see me?"

Juniper was opening her mouth to tell her about the hot-air balloon, when Quirky Sue shook her head.

"I guess it doesn't matter how," Sue said. "And really, it's not some deep, dark secret. It's just Hannah's always thought I was bad at my job or wasn't working hard enough." Her voice shook, but so far there weren't any tears. "I'm the one waking up before sunrise to make breakfast for all the guests, but if I try to take a break after being up for twice as long as Hannah, she makes comments like I have a bad work ethic." Quirky Sue shook her head. "I just didn't want to deal with another fight."

"So you were lying to Hannah?" Britt asked when I didn't say anything.

Quirky Sue's lip trembled. "You must think I'm terrible."

Juniper was at Sue's side and gave her a half hug. "We never said that."

"Thank you." Quirky Sue's eyes squeezed shut. "We all loved Rose, but now that she's gone, it's like none of them miss her. Sometimes I just need to walk through the vineyard and process everything, since none of them want to talk about her."

What she was saying made sense. While I realize it's judgmental to accuse Hot Hannah of being judgmental, I could absolutely imagine a world where Sue felt the need to lie about taking a walk to keep Hot Hannah from making snide comments.

"And the rosé?" I asked. "Why did you set out the wrong bottle?"

"I'm so sorry." Quirky Sue's eyes turned pleading, and you'd think I'd just accused her of murder.

"It's fine," I said, since she was waiting for an answer.

"But why was the bottle out?" Juniper prodded when Sue didn't say anything else.

"Oh, right." Quirky Sue tried to stand up a little straighter, but it somehow made her look more defeated. "I lost track of time walking through the vineyard. When I saw how late it was, I was far away from the winery. I had to rush back to get everything set up, and I was in such a hurry, I must've grabbed the wrong bottle."

"Thank you for clearing that up," Juniper said with an encouraging smile. I'd meant to thank her, but I'd kind of slumped against the couch and wasn't ready to talk.

Quirky Sue nodded, but instead of looking relieved, there was something like fear in her eyes. "You won't tell Hannah?"

"Of course not," Juniper promised for all of us. "We're so thankful for how hard you've worked to make this stay enjoyable. We'd never do anything to cause you trouble."

"Okay." Quirky Sue took a deep, quivering breath. "Was there anything else you needed?"

Juniper looked at me, and I shook my head. "Nope," my sister said. "That'll be all. Thanks again for clearing up that confusion."

"My pleasure," Quirky Sue said, her answer seeming more out of habit than from genuine pleasure. She left right after and, if I had to guess, hurried downstairs so Juniper couldn't stop her a second time.

"Well, that clears that up," Britt said, smoothing some of the hair off my forehead.

"Yeah," I said, eyeing the quilt. I was still trapped, and I needed coffee. But the effort it would take to get up felt like a lot.

Before I mustered the energy, Juniper brought me a hot cup of coffee, along with my phone. As if by magic, the phone lit up with Mom's number the moment it touched my hand.

"Figures," I said, showing the screen to Britt. I never could figure out how Mom had sonar for when I was in trouble, but ignoring her calls would only make her call more. Answering the phone, I started speaking before she could talk. "Hi, Mom. Yes, I went to the ER for carbon dioxide poisoning, but I'm fine now. They discharged me, I took a nap, and now I'm having coffee."

The silence on the other end of the line stretched on for so long, I checked to make sure the call hadn't disconnected. Then Mom said, "Well, Holt, I actually called to ask about Christmas."

Uh-oh.

Smoothing out my tousled hair, I asked, "So Juniper didn't send any photos of me looking...purple?"

"No. No, she did not." Mom's voice was clipped. Was she upset about my ER visit or the fact moving to Australia had dulled her superpower?

Juniper sat on the floor with Chouzie in her lap watching me flounder like it was her favorite reality show. And Juniper was getting all this entertainment just from my end of the call; it's not like Mom was on speaker.

"Okay, so..." I didn't know what to say next.

Her voice grew muffled, and it sounded like Mom was giving Dad a status update.

When Mom returned to the phone she was all business. "What about your girlfriend? Is Brittany still there?"

"Um." I glanced at Britt, wondering if she could hear Mom. "Yes."

"Is she taking good care of you?"

I wanted to say Britt forced me into a car and brought me to the hospital, but I had a suspicion Mom would take Brittany's side, so instead I said, "Yes."

There was another muffled conversation with Dad. "Do you need any help?"

"Nope. Thirty-year-old adult over here. I'm fine."

"Promise?"

My cheeks began heating. I should have taken the call in my bedroom. This wasn't a conversation I needed Britt or Juniper overhearing. "Yeah, I promise."

"Okay. Then, if you're sure you don't need us, we'll stay in Australia."

Had she seriously thought about flying out? Trying to put a little more energy in my voice, I said, "Yup, I'm fine, or great. Super. Don't worry about me."

"All right." Mom didn't sound fully convinced. "Get some rest. We'll talk about Christmas some other time."

"Sure." I sighed, so exhausted from Quirky Sue and the call with Mom, I could have fallen back asleep before the call ended.

"Holt, I love you."

I glanced at Brittany, suddenly alert. I'm an adult. It shouldn't be embarrassing to tell my mom I love her. Still, I said, "Yeah. You too."

Brittany and Juniper both cringed like an air-raid siren had gone off. Bad move.

"I love you too," I added quickly, before hanging up.

"That was close," Juniper said, standing. "I'll take Chouzie out, so you two can have a minute. But when I come back, I'm eating food."

Brittany's eyes twinkled. "It's a date."

While Juniper got Chouzie's leash on, I scrolled through my phone's notifications. I'd missed an earlier call from Mom. There was a text from Darren with a list of local lawyers and the explanation of: *Just in case you're arrested...* But the surprise was a photo from Juniper. It was a close-up of me sleeping in Brittany's lap. It was just my face and our hands interlaced, with my hospital bracelet in focus. The photo was almost artsy.

I showed it to Brittany as soon as Juniper left—no need to inflate my sister's ego. "I kind of like this."

"Do you?" Britt's voice was soft.

"Yeah. My muscles look amazing. Do you see all those veins?"

Britt gave me a playful shove, and I rolled, groaning to the other side of the couch. Then I remembered I still had coffee, and drinking coffee was a higher priority than flirting. After taking a few long gulps, I set the mug down. Juniper probably expected me and Britt to have some sort of heart-to-heart about how life is fleeting and all that junk, but I had other things on my mind.

"Was Brad really the one to pull me out of the vat?"

"Oh." Britt's face scrunched up.

That was the wrong thing to say. I needed more coffee. I was bungling this.

Taking Britt's hand, I decided to go the Juniper route. "I mean, thank you for all of your"—I almost said *love*, but Britt and I weren't there yet—"your support today. I truly appreciate it."

That's when Brittany burst out laughing—this is why I don't bother being nice. "How many seminars do they make you take at work?"

"Enough," I said. Then I winked. "I have a certificate that states I'm qualified to speak with hostile clients and coworkers."

"Good to know," Britt said.

I attempted to smooth out my hair. I could tell it was in bad enough shape that I'd need a mirror and product to fix it.

It took some effort, but I got up and draped the quilt against the couch. There was a folded washcloth on Brittany's lap. I frowned. "What's that for?"

"Uh...nothing."

I waited.

"It was Juniper's suggestion when you started drooling."

"Umm..." Heat flooded my cheeks. I opened my mouth and closed it again, since the only thing I'd say would be a snarky comment. I shook my head. "I'm going to go freshen up. Am I allowed to lock the door?"

"If you promise not to pass out."

I raised my right hand. "Swear."

By the time I'd washed my face (Britt hadn't been kidding about the drool) and styled my hair, the rest of the group was back in our suite.

Sienna was waiting near the door. Before I could get very far, she was standing in front of me. She went up on tippy-toes, cupped my face with her hand, and gently pulled so I was at her eye level.

Huh. I guess I hadn't seen Sienna since before my wine bath. She'd missed the trip to the ER.

I tried to grin. "How do I look?"

She didn't answer immediately, just kept my face pulled near hers, looking me over. Finally satisfied, she let go, and I stood up straight. "Not great," she said. "But better than you were in July."

"Thanks," I said a little sarcastically. Still, at least I was in better shape than in the summer.

Britt was still on the couch. I was about to join her, but Juniper distracted me. She was pinching my wallet between her thumb and finger, peering at it like it was an alien artifact.

"What are you doing?" I asked.

"Just thinking."

"Okay, then give me my wallet."

She tossed it at me, and I struggled to catch it. I was a lot better after my nap, but my reflexes were delayed.

"What I wondered," Juniper said, once I'd shoved the wallet into my pocket like nothing had happened, "is your wallet was at the winery for so long. Someone could have stolen stuff or planted something."

I scrubbed a hand across my face. Why did I keep getting into these messes? Sitting at the kitchenette, I thumbed through my wallet. Everything appeared to be as I had left it. Then on a hunch, I counted the cash. "Everything's here except for the twenty you stole from me."

Juniper did a little dance. "Excellent work." She handed me the missing bill. "Brittany said you were doing better. But I wasn't sure."

I leaned back in the kitchen chair. "So you decided thieving was your best option?"

Juniper tossed her hair. "It worked didn't it?"

Paul joined me at the table. "Was anything planted?"

"Is this another test?"

He shook his head. "No, this is me making sure you're not wrongfully arrested with incriminating evidence found in your pocket."

One look at Paul's serious face had me digging through my wallet again.

"See if there's a receipt for corkscrews," Juniper suggested, leaning over my chair.

"Nope," I said. "No receipts or smoking guns. Sorry, sis. I think you're the only one who's been tampering."

"Let me see your phone," Paul said.

I handed it over, and everyone watched as he popped the phone out of the case, removed the back panel, and finally the battery. After a brief examination, he seemed to be satisfied and put the pieces back together.

"Unlock it for me."

I did as requested, and Paul proceeded to check my settings and user history. Then he nodded. "You should be good."

"Wait!" Juniper was having way too much fun with this. "We haven't checked your shoes. They could have put a bug or a GPS tracker in there."

Next thing I knew, Juniper was shoving her hands into my shoes and feeling around.

"Ew. Juniper, that's disgusting."

Juniper kept searching.

Resting my head in my hand, I said, "Please stop."

Juniper ignored me.

Grimacing, I shifted in my chair. It was all so sickening. I tried again to get Juniper to stop. "Come on," I said. "If it was one of the managers, they could have bugged the whole suite while we were gone."

Juniper pointed a shoe at me. "No need to get all paranoid."

I raised my arms. "I'm not the one who's paranoid."

"Wait, I feel something." Juniper scrunched her nose as she began removing her hand. For a second she looked triumphant. "See. I found a...piece of gravel wrapped in lint."

"Nice work," I said. "Now put the shoes down."

"Hold on." Juniper flipped the shoes over and began examining the treads. "Nothing here," she reported. "We'll have to cut open the soles to take a look. Where's a good knife?"

"I've got one here," Paul said, his eyes twinkling the way Britt's did.

"Don't encourage her," I groaned.

Paul opened up a heavy-duty pocketknife and held it out to Juniper.

She hesitated.

Ordinarily, I'd have chased Juniper around the couch until I'd reclaimed my shoes. But after the day's misadventure, if I started running, there was a decent chance I'd pass out. So I watched from my seat.

Would Juniper actually cut my shoes open if I didn't stop her?

Slowly, Juniper took the knife.

"Paul!" both Brittany and Sienna yelled.

He shrugged. Paul was as curious as I was to see what Juniper would do.

"Okay," Juniper said. "I'm going to cut your shoe open to look for a bug."

Everyone was watching Juniper, and at least I was holding my breath.

"So, here I go." Juniper held the blade by the shoe. "I'm going to start cutting." She held her hand there, poised for action a moment longer, then dropped the shoe and handed the knife back to Paul. The room took a collective inhale.

"Fine." Juniper rolled her eyes. "I can't actually cut open your shoes. Are you happy now?"

"Delighted," I said, sitting back. "Now, if you could go wash the foot gunk off your hands—"

What had I done? I should have known better. Juniper began advancing with her hands outstretched. "Why. Did I touch something gross?"

"Juniper," I said, shifting in my chair.

"Careful," Brittany warned right before Juniper lunged for me.

In reality, Juniper was only playing and was too far away to reach me, but I acted on instinct. Jumping from my spot, I ran around the table, which was more movement than my body could handle. Suddenly the kitchen fell away. There was rushing in my ears and blackness like I was deep underwater.

Something grabbed at me, and I groaned.

"I've got him," a deep voice said.

"Holt, can you hear me?"

It was Brittany. When I opened my eyes, instead of seeing blackness, I was back in the kitchenette with Paul and Brittany holding on to either side of me.

There was a strangled gasp, and after verifying I hadn't made the sound, I found Juniper white-faced on the other end of the table. She began moving toward me, and I flinched. Weren't her hands gross?

A woman's voice so deep I didn't recognize it said, "Go get cleaned up." The voice had come from beside me. Wasn't Brittany beside me? Checking, there was Britt, her face dark with anger.

When Juniper stayed frozen to her spot, Brittany said in her extra-deep voice, "He was in the hospital today. What were you thinking?"

Juniper let out a cry before running into the bathroom. Paul let out a low whistle.

"Not now," Brittany snapped. "Let's get him to the couch."

"I can walk," I said, trying to struggle out of their grasp.

"Then let's go," Paul said. We made it to the couch, neither one of them letting go until I was safely deposited. Probably a good thing they came along. I was able to hold my weight but had difficulty walking a straight line...Probably too much wine.

I rested my eyes for a moment, and when I opened them, Britt, Paul, and Sienna were all standing over me with worried faces.

"Should we take him back to the hospital?" Paul asked.

"I'm fine," I said, sounding like a whiny child.

We all looked at Brittany. If she decided on the hospital, Paul would be hauling me back to his Subaru, and I'd be getting a matching ER bracelet.

"We'll stay." Brittany's voice was still too deep. She glared at the bathroom door. "We'll see how Holt is later."

"Okay," Sienna said, twirling a dreadlock between her fingers. "Well, Paul and I were thinking about making tonight a game night. They have lots of options downstairs. Holt, is there anything you'd want to play?"

Honestly, probably not, but Sienna was giving me an opportunity to let things return to normal, so I attempted a grin. "I like poker."

Paul bent to give my shoulder a gentle clap. "Yeah, you do."

"Be back in five," Sienna called as she and Paul left.

Brittany sat next to me, glowering at nothing in particular. This was uncharted territory. I'd never seen Britt mad—at least she wasn't mad at me.

Leaning against her, I said, "I'm all right. Just a little dizzy."

"You nearly hit your head on the table. If Paul hadn't…" She twisted to face me. "Do you know the kinds of calls I've gotten from people who *actually* hit their heads the way you *almost* did?"

"I'm okay," I repeated.

"But you almost weren't."

I didn't know what to say, so I didn't say anything. Instead, I wrapped my arms around her and hoped I was doing the right thing. At first she tensed up, but then her arms went around me, and she buried her face in my chest. She wasn't crying, but she held on like I could disappear.

It was one of those heartwarming greeting card moments, until my stomach growled. A muffled giggle came from Brittany, and she sat up, looking more herself. "Let's see what kind of food Sue brought us."

CHAPTER 8

Britt insisted on fixing me a plate and having me eat on the couch. To be fair, I didn't fight her very hard on this. I didn't eat much, and Brittany took my plate away when I began playing with my food.

"You know, no one would be upset if you decided not to play poker."

"Ouch," I said.

Brittany made a face. "You know what I meant. You could go to bed early or watch a movie."

Taking Britt's hand, I pulled her onto my lap. "I'm onto you," I whispered. "You can't bluff, and you're afraid you'll lose."

Before Britt could answer, the bathroom door opened and the bedroom door shut.

I rested my head back. This was proving to be one exhausting day. "I should talk to Juniper."

"Eh," Brittany said.

"I *shouldn't* talk to her?"

Britt shifted on my lap, some of her anger resurfacing. "What she did was really bad. She should feel guilty enough that she bothers to learn from her mistake."

"What, so she won't chase me the next time I jump into a pool of carbon dioxide?"

"Something like that."

"How many vats do you think I'll jump into?"

Brittany smiled, but it didn't reach her eyes. "Hard to say." She gave me a quick kiss and then headed to the kitchenette, where she stayed, putting away leftovers and tidying until Paul and Sienna returned.

"Sorry it took so long," Paul said. "We had to combine like five different decks of cards to make a full deck."

They joined Britt in the kitchenette, and I wondered if I'd have to leave the couch to play poker. Unexpectedly, Britt came by with a fresh plate of food. "Here. Go talk to your sister. She hasn't eaten since the patio tasting." Brittany sighed. "She watched you sleep just as much as I did. It's been a challenging day for all of us."

I got up carefully, with Brittany hovering beside me and Paul a couple of steps away. When I was almost at the girls' room, I took the plate from Brittany, then knocked.

The only answer I got was a growl from Chouzie.

"Juniper?" I asked, slowly opening the door. There was a snuffle that sounded more human than dog. "I'm coming in," I announced, before pausing, giving her one last chance to tell me to get lost.

Growing up, we'd had a pet goldfish who died when Juniper was around five. I'd found her all red-faced and snotty, crying on the pantry floor in one of her princess costumes when all I'd wanted was a snack.

That's what she reminded me of as she sat on the trundle bed, her knees pulled up against her stomach, Chouzie sitting beside her as an honor guard. My sister with runway looks after getting out of bed, the woman who could shed graceful tears during sad movies, had been ugly crying.

"I brought some supper," I said, closing the door.

With that, Juniper burst into another round of tears.

What had I done? I glanced at the door, wishing I was on the other side of it.

I hadn't been very understanding when Juniper was sad about the goldfish, but I'd been a kid at the time. This would be different.

Sitting beside her on the trundle bed, I stayed quiet, waiting for her tears to run their course.

While I didn't have a stopwatch tracking how long I waited for her to calm down, I did wait for a long time. Once, I put a hand on her back, but when she started crying harder, I took my hand away.

So I wasn't exactly hungry, but I was sitting on a trundle bed next to a crying woman and a plate of food. At a certain point, boredom took over, and I reached for a slice of bread.

"Don't eat my food," Juniper said.

I half smiled. "I didn't think you were hungry."

"Of course I'm hungry," Juniper said. "I haven't eaten all day."

A bit of an exaggeration, but I let it go. "Then here," I said, handing over the plate.

I rested my eyes, while Juniper scarfed down the food. Once she'd finished, Juniper set her head on my shoulder. "I'm sorry," she said. "I wasn't thinking."

"It's all right."

We sat like that for so long my breathing began to grow heavy. Then Juniper sat up, making a sound that was part snuffle, part giggle. "I've never seen Brittany so upset."

I tried not to grin. "Yeah, neither have I."

"She really likes you."

Warmth spread through my body. "I guess so."

Juniper surprised me by taking my hand. "I don't know what I was thinking," she said again. "I've been off this trip. Jude couldn't come, and I know I shouldn't be jealous, but I haven't loved being the fifth wheel on my own vacation. Still, I shouldn't have been such a brat."

"You know, Juniper," I said, "I'm pretty used to you being a brat."

"Hey!" Juniper punched my shoulder. "Well, I'm pretty used to you being a butt."

I shrugged. "I guess that makes us even."

Something dark flashed through her eyes. Possibly a memory. Just how close had I been to hitting my head on the table?

"Ugh." Juniper began wiping under her eyes. "I don't know how I'm supposed to go out there and face everyone."

I decided against making a joke about helping Juniper escape out the window.

"Come on," I said. "It's fine. It's just my girlfriend and her family. What could they do?"

"Brittany hates me," Juniper said. Her mouth began trembling, and I was in danger of experiencing another round of crying.

"She doesn't hate you," I said. "It was her idea that I bring you food. It's been a scary day for all of us. We need to cut each other some slack."

"But I almost killed you!" And with that Juniper began weeping. I thought I'd sounded so calm and mature, yet if I'd done my job, my sister wouldn't be hysterical.

Since being nice hadn't worked, I waited until Juniper's crying had slowed to do what I do best—be a butt.

"Do you have your phone?" I asked.

"Yeah" came her trembling reply. "Why?"

"Because mine's in the living room, and I need photo evidence of the one time you didn't look perfect."

"Holt!" That shocked the sorrow out of her.

"It won't even make us even. Think of all the horrible pictures you have of me."

Juniper thought this through, then took out her phone, some of her usual bounce returning to her voice. "It can't be that bad." She turned the camera to selfie mode, then dropped her phone with a gasp. "Gross! I'm all red and puffy."

I grinned. "Yup."

Juniper stuck her tongue out at me but was a good enough sport to take several photos of the two of us. She sent them all to me, then had me wait while she fixed her face in the room's vanity—yet another reason the girls' room was so much nicer than mine.

"Okay," she said, looking remarkably better. "Let's go."

No one made a big deal at our entrance. All Paul did was ask if we were both playing and then dealt the cards. They'd flipped over the top of the ottoman, transforming it into a table, so we could play poker on the couch.

"Tonight's just about having fun," Paul informed us. "But if we play again in the future, there will be stakes."

I covered a yawn and nodded. Britt was watching me, the scar by her eyebrow still visible, and I knew she was debating telling me to go to bed. Sitting in a corner seat on the couch with Brittany beside me, I whispered, "Relax. Blacking out is way different from passing out."

Brittany's frown deepened, but there was a faint spark in her eyes, and she didn't tell me to go to bed.

If Paul gauged my poker playing from my night's performance, he'd be in for a surprise. Tonight I really wasn't paying attention to the game. While my brain was still a little muddled and I was exhausted, the main reason I was so distracted was that I was trying to figure out who could have hit Joe and pushed him into the tank.

"Does anyone know if Joe's conscious?" I asked as I got two new cards from Paul without noticing what had previously been in my hand.

"Brad was in the lobby when we got the cards and chips," Sienna said. "Between checking in a few guests, he said Joe was spending the night in the hospital and they were hoping he'd be talking in the morning."

I nodded.

"Did he happen to say if they were new reservations, thanks to my marketing push?" Juniper asked.

"Uh, no. He didn't say," Sienna answered.

"Sure." Juniper nodded. "I was hoping my PR stuff was working."

Brittany had just folded, and I followed suit. When I tossed my cards onto the table, they landed face up.

"You had a full house?" Paul asked.

"Uh, maybe," I said, then asked Brittany, "How did Brad end up in the winery?"

"You do know how to play, right?" Paul asked.

"Yup," I said.

Paul sent Juniper a questioning look. While she'd been uncharacteristically shy at the start of the game, her competitive nature had kicked in pretty quick, and she had most of the chips piled in front of her. She raised her arms in a cartoon shrug. "He's the one who taught me to play."

"I see," Paul said. He picked up the full house almost lovingly and set it on the discard pile.

Brittany and Sienna shared a look that must've had to do with Paul's reaction to the full house. Only then did Britt answer my question. "I began running to the winery the moment I got your call." Britt's voice was quiet, and she watched me intently, like the wrong word would send me spiraling into shock. "Brad was nearby and asked what had happened. I told him there was an emergency at the winery but I didn't know what. He followed me and helped get you and Joe out of the tank."

I bent closer. "Where was he coming from? Could he be the one who pushed Joe and then escaped?"

Brittany rested a hand on my knee. "It's possible."

Before I could ask another question, Juniper asked Britt, "Are you going to tell him, or should I?"

Britt's mouth quirked. "I'll tell him."

I shifted in my seat, not enjoying the feeling of being ganged up on.

"Holt," Brittany said. "It's time for you to go to bed."

"What? Where's this coming from?" I asked.

"Well, your eyes are watering," Brittany said kindly.

"And your face is turning red," Juniper added.

"Plus," Paul said, delivering my worst sin of the night, "you folded with a full house."

I wanted to argue, wanted more time to discuss theories about Brad, but that wouldn't happen. My friends were cutting me off from further sleuthing. I might as well accept my bedtime like a man instead of throwing a temper tantrum.

Brittany took my arm and walked me to my room. Juniper had gone ahead and turned a lamp on, then folded back the comforter. I'd forgotten about my unicorn princess bedding and was tempted to retrieve the blue quilt from the couch. In the end I decided that would be too much work. When I got into bed, there was a plastic crinkling.

Britt tilted her head. "Is that...?" She turned to Juniper. "Did you make them put a potty-proof cover over Holt's mattress?"

Juniper shifted on her feet, still a little skittish around my girlfriend. "Uh, yeah."

Britt's eyes danced with amusement. "How thoughtful."

"Whose side are you on?" I growled.

Brittany smoothed my hair back, and my eyes drooped shut. "If you need a mattress protector, you need a mattress protector. There's no shame in that."

I struggled to sit up. "But I don't need a mattress protector."

Brittany winked. "Of course you don't."

"Be nice," I grumbled, rolling onto my side. "I was in the hospital today."

"Okay," Britt said, right as Juniper said, "No promises."

Juniper gave a self-conscious laugh before kissing my forehead. "I love you," she said.

Remembering the day's earlier mistake with Mom, I said, "I love you too."

Brittany waited for Juniper to leave, before settling the comforter over me. "Good night, mister," she said.

"You're leaving?" I asked, raising my head. Then, remembering I was a grown man who didn't need someone holding his hand to fall asleep, I said the only thing that popped into my head. "I haven't brushed my teeth."

Brittany sat on the edge of the bed. "I think you can skip that for one night."

"Are you sure?" I yawned, settling deep into the pillow. "Good hygiene is one of the main things people look for in a partner."

Britt gave a light laugh. "Well, if I break up with you tomorrow, you'll know why."

She must've waited until I was asleep—not that she had long to wait. I don't remember her leaving, or Paul snoring, or anything at all until I woke up with the sun streaming across the room and a policeman outside my door.

CHAPTER 9

To be fair, I didn't know that Cop Kid was outside my door when I woke up. While I saw him in the kitchenette, talking to Juniper on my way to the bathroom, my focus had been on showering and brushing my teeth. I'd skipped the toothbrush last night, and though I'm pretty sure Britt was joking, I didn't want to push my luck on the hygiene front.

I didn't process what Cop Kid's presence symbolized until halfway through my shower—I can't be considered smart until after a few doses of caffeine. Cop Kid was still in the main room when I left the bathroom, but he'd moved from the kitchenette with Juniper to the couch with Brittany.

Brittany. Had I said anything stupid last night? I couldn't remember.

I went to the Keurig and set up a cup of coffee, trying to be as unobtrusive as possible. This was my riskiest maneuver, but I needed coffee more than I needed to avoid a morning conversation with the police. Besides, if Cop Kid really needed to talk to me, he'd find me sooner or later.

My jaw ticked as footsteps approached. "It's good to see you this morning," the officer said. The weird thing is he seemed to mean it. The way he behaved, you'd think we were buddies.

"Morning," I said, wondering if there was anything in the constitution about not questioning suspects until they're fully caffeinated—I should ask my buddy Darren.

"How are you feeling?" he asked.

I raised my eyebrows. "Do you care?"

"Holt." Brittany widened her eyes, presumably trying to signal for me to behave.

Cop Kid waved a hand. "It's fine. Now, I'm sorry to have to do this with you right after you woke up, but I didn't think you'd sleep in so late."

"Yeah, well, almost dying is pretty exhausting."

"Mm-hmm," Cop Kid said, covering his mouth with a hand. After a moment he cleared his throat, and when he moved his hand away, he almost looked serious. "Is this a good place to talk?"

Brittany and Juniper were on the couch, pretending not to eavesdrop. Having to talk to the police was one thing, but going through the whole experience with my sister and girlfriend listening was another.

After locating my sunglasses on the counter, I headed to the door with my coffee. "I need some air."

Brittany half stood. "Can you walk?"

"Yeah." I tried not to sound annoyed. "I'm fine."

The worry scar was back. "That's what you said last night."

Cop Kid looked between us. "Don't worry," he said, almost sounding responsible. "I'll keep an eye on him."

We walked down to the patio. Choosing a semi-reclined chair, I let out a sigh, glad to be off my feet. I expected Cop Kid to launch into a round of questions, but he seemed happy to enjoy the weather. In the sunlight, Cop Kid's face showed faint wrinkles.

"How old are you?" I asked.

Cop Kid nodded like he'd expected the question. "I'm thirty-three."

"But then...you're older than me?"

"I guess so," he said, not at all bothered by my questions.

"It's just, you look so..."

"Young?" He smirked. "I still get carded at bars."

"Makes sense."

Cop Kid didn't immediately say anything else, and I took a few gulps of coffee as I waited. I'm pretty sure he was figuring out the best way to bring up yesterday's wine bath.

"I spoke with Joe Shaw this morning," he said.

"Oh?" I leaned toward Cop Kid—though his nickname no longer worked, given his advanced years. Problem was, I had no idea what Cop Kid's real name was. "Did Joe say who pushed him?"

Cop Kid watched me intently as he said, "Joe thinks you did it."

"What!" I stood up and began pacing. "What?" I paused in front of the cop. "Me? *I pushed him?* He said I pushed him?"

Cop Kid was also on his feet. "Whoa, slow down." He gestured to my seat. "Take a moment. We'll work through this."

"Yeah! You already think I murdered my ex-girlfriend. Now someone I risked my life for is saying I'm the one who tried to kill him."

"Sit. Down."

I sat. Tugging at my hair, I said, "I was with Juniper. I called Brittany the moment there was trouble."

"Holt, I need you to take some deep breaths."

It was said with a forced calmness. A tone I'd heard before. I crossed my arms. "You sound like Britt."

"If you don't calm down, we'll need to call her."

"Fine," I muttered. Though having a paramedic girlfriend was proving to be rather inconvenient.

Stopping mid-freak-out, with the cop who might arrest you and is threatening to call your girlfriend, is easier said than done. Plus, the guy seemed amused by the conflicting emotions flashing across my face.

"Jerk," I muttered.

Cop Kid smiled. "Glad to see you're more yourself. Now, are you ready to have an actual conversation?"

What was that supposed to mean? When I didn't say anything, Cop Kid sat back in his chair and took out his notebook. He began flipping through pages before glancing up at me. "Between you and me, we think it's unlikely you killed Natasha. We've found no evidence of you attempting to keep in touch after your breakup. The blood on your clothes was consistent with her falling into your arms. And you weren't kidding; she'd changed a lot after college."

"Thank you." I let out a breath I didn't know I'd been holding in. "That's what I keep telling people."

"Now, do you have any idea why Joe would accuse you?"

"No." I shook my head. "I've barely seen the guy. What did he say exactly?"

"He said you followed him into the winery; then he woke up in the hospital bed and assumed you pushed him."

Great.

I shifted in my seat. "He was talking to someone. I heard voices before the splash. That's the person who pushed him."

"Joe says he doesn't remember talking to anyone."

I stood up again, getting excited. "He's lying."

"That's a possibility," Cop Kid said carefully. "The doctor also said memory loss is common surrounding traumatic events."

Rubbing a hand over my face, I said, "I can't believe this."

Something in Cop Kid's face gave the impression he found it all funny. "You've had quite the weekend," he said dryly.

I glared at him, and he raised his hands defensively. "Sorry. I need you to think carefully. When you were in the winery and heard talking, was Joe speaking to a man or a woman? Did you catch any words?"

I closed my eyes, trying to relive the moment. Yet in my memory, it was all so muffled and echoey. I shook my head. "I don't know. But"—I glanced around the patio to make sure no one was listening—"Brad was by the winery when it happened."

"I see," Cop Kid said.

One look from him had me realizing what I'd done. I'd been mad at Joe for accusing me after I'd rescued him, and I'd turned around and done the exact same thing to Brad.

Mom would be proud.

CHAPTER 10

Brittany, Juniper, and Chouzie were waiting in the lobby of Rose's Repose when Cop Kid brought me back.

Juniper put a hand on her hip. "What, no handcuffs?"

"Not yet," I grumbled.

Cop Kid shared a professional nod with Brittany. "I brought him back in one piece."

"Thank you," she said.

Cop Kid said goodbye, and we all waited to discuss his visit until his car had left the parking lot.

"Phew," Juniper said. "That was a close one. Did you know this morning he kept asking me if I was sure we'd entered the winery at the same time and never separated? When I said I was sure, he asked if I'd lie for you."

"What did you say?" I asked.

"Oh, you know." Juniper tossed her hair. "I lied and said no."

"Juniper, you could go to jail for lying."

"Just like you could go to jail for murder and attempted murder."

"Enough!" Brittany said.

Juniper and I shared a look. Maybe we should tone down the sibling shenanigans until Britt had more time to process what happened yesterday.

"Do you want breakfast?" Britt asked. "They stopped serving it, but I saved you a plate."

I shook my head. "All I need is more coffee."

"Here." Juniper took my empty mug and disappeared into the dining area.

"Where are Paul and Sienna?" I asked.

"They're taking a long walk and having brunch out in the vineyard."

There went Paul, proving again how romantic he was. I slid an arm around Britt's side. "Sorry this trip hasn't been very relaxing. Truth be told, I don't think I'm a vineyard guy."

Brittany leaned against me. "I can understand why after that rosé Paul gave you."

My laugh came out as a low rumble. "True. This trip would have been perfect, if not for that rosé."

As I tightened my arm around Britt, I remembered the wine. What was the deal with the rosé? And why were there so many attacks at the winery?

I shifted to look down at Britt. "Maybe we can have our own romantic picnic on the grounds, but nearby...like in view of the winery?"

"Is this an actual date or undercover work?" Juniper had returned unnoticed with my coffee. "Because if it's part of the case, Chouzie and I are coming too."

I glanced at Britt, then said, "Sure," before realizing I'd agreed to share a picnic blanket with Brittany, Juniper, and Chouzie.

"We'll need to get food and a blanket," Britt said.

"Sounds good," I said. But I was still being treated like a delicate flower about to wilt in the sunshine. Because I wasn't allowed to get anything for *my* picnic. Juniper gave me Chouzie's leash and told me to keep an eye on him, while she went upstairs to get a picnic blanket and travel cups and Brittany went to the kitchen to get the food.

Sitting down in an armchair next to the shelf of games, Chouzie lay protectively beside me, even resting his head on my feet. Leaning over, I scratched his fur. Could Chouzie have been worried about me?

Thinking no one was around, I told him, "I'm okay, buddy."

Then I heard "I hope you're feeling better" and realized Hot Hannah had just walked in.

I sat up immediately, not loving being caught talking to a dog. I cleared my throat and said, "Much better, thank you."

"It was such surprising news," Hannah said, kneeling in front of me in her high heels and petting Chouzie, who stiffened at her touch. "What were you even doing in the winery?"

Huh. She'd asked the question casually enough, but her voice had changed, like she was trying too hard to sound casual. This was the real reason she was checking up on me. For some reason she needed to know what I'd been doing in the winery. I settled for the half-truth I'd told the cop. "After Joe took us grape picking, Juniper and I had a couple of follow-up questions and saw Joe going into the winery."

"You shouldn't have been in there without a chaperone," Hannah said, wobbling a little as she stood up.

I raised an eyebrow. It wasn't like I expected a parade for saving Joe, but Hannah's lack of enthusiasm was definitely suspicious.

Hot Hannah came to that realization a moment after me. "But"—she readjusted her skirt—"that little indiscretion saved Joe's life, so good job," and she patted my knee before walking away.

That had been very unpleasant. Why had she petted me like I was a dog?

"Why's your face green?" Juniper asked. "Wait." Her voice changed from curious to concerned. "Are you going to be sick?" Dropping a large tote bag, Juniper found a trash can and rushed to my side.

"Slow down. I'm good."

I grinned to prove the point, but Juniper wrinkled her nose and moved the garbage can closer to my face. "Then why are you grimacing?"

Which was the perfect time for Brittany to walk in. She dropped her basket and was by my side, checking my pulse and pupils. Honestly, you end up in an ER and almost fall into a table and everyone thinks you're made of glass.

I would have made a getaway, but I was trapped in my seat by two women and a dog. I began swatting their hands away. "Space," I said. "I need space."

The moment I had room, I was out of the chair and running outside.

"He's going to be sick," I heard Juniper say just as I slammed the front door shut.

I was leaning against the porch railing when Juniper and Brittany appeared with their bags and Chouzie.

"What happened while we were gone?" Brittany asked. She was clearly worried, but at least she wasn't overcrowding me.

"Hannah came by. She told me the winery was off-limits, then thanked me for saving Joe, and..." I trailed off. Would this be another thing Juniper would tease me about?

"And?" Juniper asked.

I fought the urge to dry heave. "And then she patted my knee."

Brittany looked confused, but Juniper said, "Ew," and gave a little shudder.

Before anyone could get any new ideas about checking on me, I reached for Brittany's picnic basket and said, "Let's go."

We did leave, but neither Brittany nor Juniper let me carry their picnic equipment. I was allowed full control of Chouzie's leash, and they mostly didn't hover.

Juniper led the way through the garden path. "I found a good spot to watch the winery this morning when I was walking Chouzie. Here." Juniper showed me a selfie she'd taken with an excellent view of the garage doors and one of the side doors.

"Works for me," I said.

When we reached the site, Juniper made us wait until she set up a Hallmark-ready picnic, then filmed herself talking about how wonderful Rose's Vineyard was for picnicking.

"You done?" I finally asked, swaying a little on my feet.

"Yes. Sorry, but some of us have to work during this free vacation."

"And how's that going for you?" I asked, getting myself settled on the blanket.

"It's been going great, Holt. Thanks for asking."

I raised an eyebrow while Brittany asked, "Really?"

"Actually, yes," Juniper said, as we began eating. "I asked this morning, and they've had a spike in reservations since we came."

"Congrats," I said.

Britt nodded in agreement before asking, "What are we looking for?"

"Something suspicious," Juniper said.

Brittany's eyes hardened, but she didn't say anything.

"Proof Brad was the one who pushed Joe," I said. "Joe must've figured out that Brad killed Tasha. They must've argued, and Brad tried to silence him. I'm pretty sure Brad does the books, so there was no reason for him to be by the winery yesterday afternoon."

"Uh, Holt," Britt said.

As if on cue, Brad had approached from the tasting room and office building. He glanced around but didn't see us on the ground in the garden. Instead of going into the winery to do something nefarious, he gave one last look at the tasting room, then ducked behind the side of the building so he wasn't visible from the tasting room. Then he lit a cigarette.

"Britt." I shook my head. "Is that where you found him?"

She nodded.

"Was he smoking?" I asked.

Britt shook her head. "I didn't notice...but there may have been a smell."

"Smoking?" I said. "His secret is smoking?"

He hadn't been by the winery to kill Joe. He'd been there to sneak a cigarette.

"Mm, he's still creepy," Juniper said. "And he could still be Tasha's dad." Brushing nonexistent crumbs off her lap, Juniper stood. "Let's ask him."

Juniper was off without waiting for us to follow. Brittany had stayed with Chouzie on the blanket, while I followed Juniper at a slower pace.

Only my sister would think it was a good idea to march up to someone and ask if they'd had a secret child thirty years ago. The question was, could she pull it off?

"Oh, hi!" Juniper called as she approached.

Instantly Bad Brad was dropping and stomping on the cigarette before popping a breath mint.

He did know we could see him—right?

"How have you been holding up?" Juniper asked, glancing meaningfully at the shoe covering the cigarette.

Bad Brad's eyes tightened, and it was like peering through the layers of creepiness and seeing the shred of a real person. Brad looked up toward the sky, his eyes watering.

Don't. Start. Crying.

"It's been tough," he said, clearing his throat.

"I'm sure," Juniper said soothingly. "First your birth daughter was killed, and then one of your best friends ended up in the hospital."

"Who?" The creepiness had utterly vanished and was replaced by confusion.

"Wasn't Natasha your birth daughter?" Juniper asked innocently.

"No. She was Rose's daughter. Hold on." Brad looked between us. "Who told you she was mine? Was it Hannah?"

When we didn't answer, he took it as a yes.

Brad sighed and shook his head. "I can't believe this. So many years later, and she still doesn't believe me."

All Juniper had to do was ask "What happened?" for Bad Brad to tell us his version of events.

"Hannah and I had just gotten married, Joe was engaged to a model, and Sue was about to leave on this big travel-abroad backpacking thing, when Rose got pregnant and wouldn't tell anyone who the father was. It wrecked everything. Hannah thought it was me and kept trying to get me to admit it. Sue canceled her trip, and Joe's engagement fell through. Then Rose decided to give the baby up for adoption and buy a vineyard. And we were all just expected to get on board. But Rose had so much money. At a certain point, she trained us to dance to her tune." He shook his head. "When she died, we thought we'd get the winery. But no. She'd hired investigators to track down her daughter and left it to her."

"Who got her money?" I asked.

Juniper elbowed me in the ribs. Apparently for her magic to work, I wasn't allowed to talk.

Brad frowned as his eyes focused on me, but he answered the question. "She was very generous with us. But"—he sighed—"Rose's Vineyard is our home. This is where my life is. We don't want to leave." He shifted on his feet. "We were trying to buy the place from Natasha."

Chouzie barked, and Brad's gaze shifted to where the dog sat with Britt.

"Rose was one of your followers," Brad said to Juniper. "I wonder if she'd like Chouzie," he added, more to himself.

Juniper swatted my shoulder. "I told you I have a lot of followers."

Bad Brad nodded. "Once Rose got really sick, your videos were the only thing that made her smile." He shrugged. "I didn't get it, but having you here...I guess it makes sense. You're kind of like Rose."

Juniper was polite. She put a hand to her heart and said, "Thank you." But I stiffened. Was that true? Were Britt, Paul, Sienna, and I just part of Juniper's web? In photos, Juniper was usually front and center. Did that mean our group was as dysfunctional as Rose's?

"Was it Rose's idea I come here?" Juniper asked.

"No." Brad shook his head. "We sent the invitation after Rose's passing. It was Sue's idea. She thought it would honor Rose's memory if her favorite social media star came and marketed the winery."

I asked, "But why invite Juniper if the winery belonged to Tasha?"

Brad looked up to the sky. "We kind of assumed the winery was left to us. And when the will was read, the contract was already signed for Juniper's visit."

"Gotcha," I said. Like that was supposed to make sense.

A ringtone began playing. Brad took out his phone and silenced it. "If you'll excuse me, I finally got a meeting with the attorney handling

Rose's estate. Natasha dying before the will was...Well, it's caused some confusion."

Once Brad was gone, Juniper gave a celebratory twirl. "You're welcome," she said.

"Yeah, yeah," I said, giving a dismissive wave and heading back to Brittany.

Juniper caught up, then passed me to reach the blanket first. "It's not Brad," she told Brittany.

Brittany's eyes met mine with a silent question. I shrugged. "It's probably not Brad." Getting back onto the blanket, I stretched out, resting my head in Britt's lap. "And if Brad's to be believed—and he was under the influence of Juniper's magical truth serum, so it's doubtful he was lying—he's not Tasha's dad and doesn't know who is."

Britt's mouth quirked as she turned to Juniper. "What did you do to him?"

Juniper batted her eyes. "Oh, you know."

"I see," Britt said, beginning to play with my hair. "So, does this mean we think Joe was Tasha's father?"

"Joe's the most likely," I said.

"So if the killer isn't Brad or Joe, that would leave Hannah or Sue," my sister said.

"Sounds right." My eyes began to water.

"Okay," Britt said. "So, Joe figures out who killed his birth daughter and confronts either Hannah or Sue in the winery. Then the killer panics and tries to silence him?"

"I guess so." I sighed, trying to remember where each of them had gone after the tasting. "How would Joe figure it out? And why would he say I pushed him?"

"He said that?!" Juniper asked.

"Yup."

"How rude."

Brittany frowned. "I don't know. Memory loss is fairly common in cases like his, so he could be confused. But usually the memory loss is fairly short term. If he'd figured out who'd killed Tasha, you'd think he'd remember."

"We could talk to him," Juniper said, waving her hand in the direction of the parking lot.

"No," Brittany said. "Absolutely not. Believe it or not, the police are actually investigating. And Joe thinks Holt tried to kill him. The two of you aren't going to start sneaking into hospitals."

Juniper gave a pouty face, which was code for *You're no fun*. "Okayyy," she said. "We're all supposed to leave tomorrow. So there's not much time to *help* the police." She rested a manicured finger on her lips. "Now, Holt are you taking a nap, or are we going to do more detective work?"

Groaning, I raised myself from Britt's lap and rested my head in my hand. "Let's detect."

"Are you sure?" Britt's hands fluttered like she was fighting the urge to pull my head back down.

"Yeah," I said. Britt didn't relax, so I added, "Maybe you drive tomorrow, and I'll sleep in the car."

"Okay." She seemed slightly relieved but still worried.

Juniper, though, considered the matter as settled. "So, what are our next steps?"

I shrugged. "We figure out what clue we've overlooked."

A silence fell between us, and while I can't speak for Brittany or Juniper, I began replaying the events at the first tasting. There had to be something we'd missed.

"It could still be Brad," Britt finally said.

Juniper's eyes got big, but she was still too nervous around my girlfriend to contradict her.

"Anything's possible, but..." I glanced at Juniper. "I really doubt it's him."

In the new quiet, I did something drastic. I intentionally remembered the moments right before Tasha died.

There I was, getting fresh air. A woman stumbled through the doors. She was a stranger. She'd had too much to drink. Her speech was garbled. There was wine all over her sweater. Then it wasn't wine, it was blood, and the corkscrew was...

"Do we know where the corkscrew came from?" I asked.

"The one that was"—Britt hesitated—"with Tasha?"

"Yes," I said, after swallowing down a sudden wave of nausea.

"Well..." Brittany took a moment to stare up at the sky. "Didn't the handle have glass swirls on it?"

"Glass swirls?" I asked.

Britt nodded.

Juniper asked. "Like Venetian glass?"

"Maybe," I said.

"Like the Venetian glass corkscrew that Hannah and Brad bought on their thirteenth wedding anniversary?"

It was hard to know for sure; still, I said, "I think so."

Juniper's eyes were huge. "According to their story, that's one of a kind."

"So if it was Hannah and Brad's one-of-a-kind corkscrew, it was in the tasting room minutes before Tasha's death?" Britt asked.

"Hold on," I said. "Why would anyone bother bringing a corkscrew from the tasting room to the winery? If I planned on murdering someone, a corkscrew wouldn't be my weapon of choice."

"What weapon would you choose?" Juniper asked.

"None of your business," I said.

Brittany was still focused on the task at hand and said, "When we were in the winery, Hannah showed us a door that led to where they stored their bottled wine."

"So?" Juniper asked.

I sat up and rubbed my eyes, trying to think it through. "I decide to have an emergency glass of wine from a bottle that's not in the tasting rooms. I take a corkscrew with me to open the bottle. I get to the winery and discover Tasha, Rose's daughter and heir to the estate, and then I stab her?" I scratched my head. "That sounds a little funny."

"It is if you word it like that," Juniper said, and Chouzie barked his agreement.

"Then what happened to the rosé? Why was it ruined?"

"Let me see." Juniper began searching on her phone. "Okay, so according to their website, Rose's Rosé is their top seller. Rose created it with blah, blah, blah processes and grapes...uh, top-secret blend..." Juniper shrugged. "Well, that was no help."

"What about Rose?" I suggested.

Brittany rested a hand on my arm. "What are you thinking?"

"She's at the heart of all this. She controlled everyone's lives like they were her chess pieces. She never corrected Hannah on her assumption that Brad had an affair. She made all her friends' lives be just so, and when she found out she was dying, she decided to leave the vineyard to a woman she's arguably never met."

"All right," Brittany said. "So you're suggesting Tasha's murder had more to do with Rose?"

"It's a theory," I said.

"Ooh." Juniper jumped to her feet. "Did someone kill Rose for the inheritance, then get a surprise when they discovered the vineyard was going to Tasha, so they killed her, too?"

Britt shook her head. "That's unlikely. Sue talked to me after breakfast this morning. She started by saying Holt was a hero and surprisingly athletic." She gave my arm a quick squeeze. "Then Sue went into great detail about Rose's illness and what her final days were like. From what Sue said, it all sounded like natural causes."

I should feel bad that Rose suffered in her final days. Still, I kind of hated her for how she'd treated her friends. And though it was unintentional, her little games may have cost Tasha her life. Which was a shame, since Tasha was a great person.

"Holt?" Juniper asked.

I blinked. "Um...let's go to the tasting room." I reached out my hand, and Juniper helped me to my feet.

Juniper's eyes widened. "You're ready to drink wine again? After yesterday, I thought it'd take you years."

I shuddered. "No, I won't be drinking. But you two can, and I'll tag along."

Brittany had been reloading the picnic supplies but said "Sure" when I caught her eye. I'd kind of forgotten about all the junk we'd hauled out for our picnic.

"I'll need to drop off Chouzie with the supplies. He's overdue for some alone time anyway..." Juniper kept chatting as she helped reload the basket and folded up the blanket with Britt.

"Holt, why don't you stay here and save yourself the extra walking?" Brittany suggested.

It was good I was wearing sunglasses so she couldn't see my eyes. Britt's comment annoyed me, but even worse, walking back to the house only to turn around and do an extended version of the same walk sounded like a lot.

"Um." I closed my eyes and took a deep breath. "Yeah. That's a good idea."

I expected Juniper to make a snarky comment, but she was watching Brittany. "Actually." She wrinkled her nose. "I just remembered I have an email from a sponsor I really need to respond to."

"Will it take long?" I asked.

Juniper tilted her head meaningfully in Britt's direction. "It'll take so long, you guys should just go to the tasting room without me. I should be done by the next adventure." With that, Juniper left loaded down with the picnic basket, blanket tote, and Chouzie's leash.

I offered Britt my arm. I'd been going for romantic but then worried Britt would take it as a sign I was unsteady on my feet.

Juniper had been right to leave. Brittany shouldn't be an afterthought. Why was it Juniper had noticed Britt was off and not me? Maybe this whole *catch the person who murdered Holt's ex-girlfriend* was getting to be too much for her.

Would it help if I invited her to Christmas? Show her how serious I was about us? Or would that be weird? It wasn't like going on a vacation with me was proving to be very relaxing.

I cleared my throat. "We can skip the tasting room. Do something more fun."

Britt nodded slowly. I could tell she was thinking, but I had no idea what was on her mind.

"Anything you want," I added. "I've been told I'm not the most romantic, which is probably why I think a murder investigation makes a good date."

Britt tugged my arm a little closer to her. "So you'd go on a hot-air balloon ride?"

"Uh..." She was probably kidding. Still, I couldn't tell from Britt's profile. But if she actually wanted a hot-air balloon, I'd get her a hot-air balloon. "Of course," I said. Letting go of her arm, I grabbed my phone. "Let's see if that place can fit us in this afternoon."

Britt didn't stop me as I did a local area search before clicking on the only option that was nearby. They had an online reservation schedule, and there was one slot still available in around ninety minutes. "We're in luck," I said, trying not to sound unexcited.

"Great," Britt said. "If they were all booked, we'd have to check for nearby skydiving."

"Or BASE jumping," I muttered, beginning to fill out the reservation info.

"Holt." Britt put a hand over my phone.

"Yeah?"

"I'm kidding. We don't need to go hot air ballooning."

I didn't want to give up too quickly, so I asked, "Are you sure?"

"I'm sure."

"Good," I breathed, putting my phone away. She'd been kidding, but her eyes weren't sparkling. Running a hand through my hair, I asked, "Is there anything I can do?"

Britt took my hand, and we walked toward the tasting room. "I'm fine."

I bumped into her. "When I said that yesterday, you made me go to the hospital."

For half a second Britt's eyes lit up, but the glimmer quickly faded. She shrugged. "I'm just tired. A lot's happened in the past two days, and I had trouble sleeping last night."

I frowned. "Why's that?"

A faint blush crept up Brittany's cheeks. "Because you were sick."

I don't know if it was the right thing to do or not, but I grinned and pulled her a little closer.

Brittany shook her head, but she seemed happier. "So, what's your plan?" she asked.

"We'll do our best to reenact the moments after the tasting."

Britt half smiled. "Including you bolting as soon as it ended?"

I opened the door for Britt and winked. "Especially that."

CHAPTER 11

The tasting room was actually fairly busy. I don't know if the reason was Juniper's social media, or because it was a Saturday, but whatever the case, most of the tables were taken.

Hannah was going with her usual tasting script and was telling cardboard stories about experiencing wine to mostly full tables while Quirky Sue made trips with bottles and platters to and from the bar. The table the five of us had taken the first day was occupied, but Britt and I got a nearby table for two.

My nose stung, and I was hit with a wave of dizziness. Somehow, while coming up with this brilliant scheme, I'd forgotten I'd be surrounded by the scent of wine.

"Holt?"

I blinked a few times before meeting Britt's eyes. "Order their newest rosé," I said.

Brittany nodded. When Hot Hannah stopped by our table, Britt did as requested. "I'd like a glass of your newest rosé."

"Oh?"

Brittany gave a serene smile. "I've been hearing such good things, but I can't remember trying it."

"Right." Hannah smoothed down her blouse before getting Britt a goblet of the pinkish liquid. "Here's our rosé from two years ago."

"Thank you." Britt swirled the goblet. "Is last year's not ready to be served?"

"Last year's is unavailable," Hannah said cryptically before leaving.

Brittany raised her eyebrows.

"She's a delight," I said.

Britt ran her finger along the rim of the goblet. "Will you be able to kiss me if I drink this?"

"That depends." Half standing, I leaned across the table and gave her a quick peck. "Does it taste like vinegar?"

Bringing the glass to her mouth, Brittany gave it a quick sniff before sipping. Her face brightened, and she smiled. "This is amazing," she said. "Like it's actually incredible. Too bad you can't try it."

I shrugged. "At least you like it."

Apparently, Rose's Rosé lived up to the hype. I frowned as a thought began to take shape. "Did Sue tell you when Rose died?"

Britt's brown eyes flicked to the ceiling for a moment. "I think it was about two months ago."

"Right," I said. "And when was she diagnosed?"

Brittany put a finger to her lips, pausing to think before she said, "A little over a year. Why? What are you thinking?"

"Hold on," I said, feeling eyes on me.

Hot Hannah was watching us and ignoring her other customers. Her face went white when I tilted my head toward our table.

"Do you need another glass?" Hannah asked as she reached us.

"No, thank you," I said, leaning back in my chair. "I was just wondering why Rose sabotaged her rosé last year."

Hannah gave a little moan and pressed her hands into our table. Instantly Brittany was on her feet, easing Hannah into her seat and shooting me a warning look.

Taking Brittany's goblet, Hannah finished the wine with a few quick gulps.

"I don't know." Hannah shook her head. "I don't know why Rose did anything. She was so spontaneous. That could be part of the fun. But it had its downsides. You never could tell what Rose would do if she got upset. We only found out after it was all bottled and a shipment was returned. She got diagnosed and just took out her frustration on the wine."

I began massaging my temples. Something wasn't clicking. "But if last year's rosé is unsellable, why was there a bottle of it at our patio tasting?"

"Oh, that." Hannah sighed. "We got rid of most of it, but Brad and the others insisted we keep a few cases. I don't know, as proof of...something."

"But why is the ruined rosé such a big secret?" I asked.

Hannah sniffed, and Britt handed her a napkin. After wiping her nose, Hannah said, "Because Rose also destroyed her records on the rosé's fermentation process."

Britt and I shared a look. I really didn't like Rose.

"It's our top seller. We can make *a rosé*, but we need *Rose's Rosé*. Losing last year's stock was one thing, but not being able to produce more..." Hannah sniffled again.

I mouthed *Wow* to Brittany.

"Is there anything you can do?" Britt asked.

"No." The word came out as a half sob. Some of the talking around us quieted as patrons looked our way. Realizing this, Hannah worked to regain some of her normal composure and stood. "We've done what we could," she said professionally. "Brad is finding a vintner to help us reverse engineer Rose's methods, and Joe's tried to do what he could." She forced a smile. "I trust this stays between us. Good day." And with that Hannah took Brittany's empty goblet and began talking to patrons at other tables, making a point of *not* looking in our direction.

Britt raised an eyebrow. "I think we've been excused."

"I guess so," I said.

We left our table just as Quirky Sue set an unopened wine bottle on the bar. On instinct, I grabbed Britt's arm, and we both watched as a corkscrew appeared. Britt's body tensed when, instead of a swirling glass inlay, the corkscrew handle was nothing but some deep mahogany.

Quirky Sue looked up and caught us staring. "Would you like a refill?"

Her question made my stomach twist...There was a chance I'd never drink wine again.

"Not a refill," Britt said and proceeded to fall silent.

Fine. I'd be the one to ask the weird question. "What happened to the Venice corkscrew?"

All the blood drained from Quirky Sue's face. "Don't you know? I thought you both saw her."

"At..." I tilted my head in the direction of the winery.

"It's just so awful." Then Quirky Sue gave a half sob and scurried away.

Brittany shook her head. "This has been quite a strain on everyone."

"What, because she's crying?" I asked while offering Britt my arm. "Don't worry. Most women can't help but cry when they get the chance to be in the same room with me."

"So you like it when women start crying?"

"Don't twist my words," I said.

I think Britt answered, but I was too busy stifling a yawn to listen.

As we left the tasting room, I asked, "How did you like your sip of wine?"

"Oh, it was phenomenal," Britt said. "We should do it again some-time."

————◦◦◦————

I was pretty worn out by the time we made it back to our rooms. The doctor had said I'd need to take it easy for a few days, but I'd hoped it was nothing a good night's sleep wouldn't fix.

I flopped onto the couch next to Juniper and let out a sigh. "Did anyone rewatch that long toast Juniper made for clues?" I asked, my eyes unusually watery. "Maybe someone took the corkscrew."

"We can do that a little later," Britt said even as Juniper closed her laptop and unlocked her phone.

"How did it go?" Juniper asked.

I was mid-yawn, so Brittany said, "I'll tell you later."

"Right," Juniper said. "Someone's had a big day."

"What's that supposed to mean?" I asked, sounding cranky.

"It means"—Brittany stood behind my spot on the couch and rested her hands on my shoulders—"even if a marching band came through here, you'd be asleep in under two minutes."

"Fiddlesticks," I said, then wondered where I'd heard that word. But when my eyes slipped shut of their own accord, I murmured, "Maybe just a quick five..."

Juniper giggled. "Or fifty."

Without looking, I could sense the glare Brittany was shooting at my sister. I smirked. My girlfriend was pretty awesome.

When I woke up, it sounded like an intense board game was being played around me.

"No, it was a new bottle," Sienna was saying. "I remember it was a new bottle, because Sue had trouble opening it and Joe had to do it."

Peeking an eye open, I found the whole crew leaning over the ottoman. The top was flipped so the hard shell was facing up. There was a collection of K-Cups around certain pieces of paper and also a random penny.

"Then what?" Brittany asked. "Do you remember the corkscrew being set down anywhere?"

"Well," Sienna said, working her dreadlocks into a braid. "I didn't see it after the Cabernet. It must have been set down behind the bar." She picked up the penny and set it behind a piece of paper and two coffee pods.

"Then anyone could have grabbed it," Paul said. He was wearing a button-up shirt with the sleeves rolled up, and his hair was falling slightly into his eyes. How was he so effortlessly handsome? In a movie, he'd be the millionaire architect, while I'd be the loser college buddy about to crash on his couch.

Paul's mouth began moving, and I realized a moment too late he was asking me, "What's wrong?"

I'd been staring. Great.

"Uh, nothing." Sitting up on the couch, I cracked my back. "Sorry."

"Here. Have some coffee," Britt said, perching on the armrest. "Since we got kicked out of the tasting room before we could do our reenactment, we're figuring it out here. We went over the speech footage. There wasn't anything incriminating, but it helped with geography."

Juniper pointed to the penny. "The last time we had a visual on the Venetian corkscrew, it was set behind the bar." This was said in the businesslike voice of a TV show detective.

"Okay." I rubbed a hand over my face, trying to clear out the cobwebs. "When the tasting ended, I left immediately."

As I spoke, Juniper moved a K-Cup of herbal tea across their little game board.

"What's that?" I asked.

Juniper beamed, like she was a genius. "It's you."

I blinked, then took a long drink of coffee. "I'm an herbal tea pod?"

"We're all represented by different types of tea," Sienna said, "and the managers are coffee pods."

"I want to be coffee," I said.

"Well, if you'd only taken a five-minute nap, you might be coffee right now," Juniper said. "But since you weren't available for questions, I went with my gut."

I raised an eyebrow. "And your gut said, *Holt's an herbal tea*?"

Juniper giggled but didn't answer the question.

"So, who was the next to leave after Holt?" Paul asked, sharing Brittany's ability to stay on topic. "Was that me?"

After they came to an agreement, another K-Cup was removed from the pretend tasting room.

"Then Hannah and Brad were talking to Juniper," Britt said. "They led us through the back and made Juniper sign a form."

"Oh, that's right," Juniper said, removing the three remaining teas and two coffees from in front of the piece of paper representing the bar. "After I signed, we went out a back door, while Brad and Hannah went up a private flight of stairs."

There were only two K-Cups remaining in the tasting room. Both were behind the bar. Both had easy access to the corkscrew. The only difference was someone had tried to kill Joe to cover up Tasha's murder. Joe must've seen Sue take the corkscrew and confronted her in the winery.

With a great deal of ceremony, Juniper picked up the penny—which I guess symbolized the corkscrew—and said, "Ladies and gentlemen, we have our killer."

CHAPTER 12

Sienna looked between us. "Now what?"

It was a fair question and one we discussed in great detail. Sue was guilty, but it's not like we could make a citizen's arrest. While Juniper's little Clue board would be enough to convict Colonel Mustard, it was pretty circumstantial for a real-life arrest.

"What happens if we call the police?" Juniper asked.

The group looked at me expectantly.

"Well, I can't call," I said. "I've already accused Brad of being the killer, and he saved my life."

"True," Paul said. "You're also the guy who didn't recognize his ex-girlfriend."

"And found both victims," Juniper added.

"The point's been made," I said a little louder than necessary. "Thank you."

Other suggestions were made, but none stuck. We were at a stalemate, and it was officially suppertime.

"Let's eat," Brittany said. "We'll think better with full stomachs."

"Hold on," Juniper said. "Doesn't Sue make the meals?"

I grimaced.

"Come on," Sienna said at the door. "She's not going to poison all of us."

She had a point. Then again, if we were getting poisoned, the wine would be the best place to hide it.

We were headed out the door, when I said, "Hey, guys, don't drink the wine tonight."

At the second-floor landing, I caught my sister fixing her hair in a hallway mirror. Her stance and the way she held her head up were like a warrior preparing for battle...But what battle did Juniper have in mind?

I grabbed her arm to keep her back from the rest of the group. "Don't do it," I whispered.

"You don't even know what I'm thinking," Juniper argued.

"I know that face. Whatever that face is thinking shouldn't be done."

"Holt," Juniper said, trying her baby-sister routine. "It's nothing dangerous. I just want a quick chat with Sue."

A headache was forming. "Juniper, please don't ask a murder suspect if they're a murderer."

"Why?" She flashed me deceptively innocent eyes. "Because you'd never do something like that?"

When I didn't answer, Juniper tilted her head toward the stairs. "Let's get supper."

She left, and I followed.

Once Juniper had made up her mind about something, it was very difficult to talk her out of it. But if I remained close, I could at least do damage control.

In the dining room, most of the tables had guests who were staying in the other rooms. I ended up sitting next to Paul and across from Brittany. As soon as Juniper and I sat down, the managers were surrounding our table. Bad Brad was pouring wine and telling Juniper how reservations were spiking. Hot Hannah, less enthusiastically, was saying the hospital had released Joe and he was back in his cottage. Quirky Sue held three plates of food and was calling me a hero. There was so much talking and movement, silverware clanking against plates, that I didn't actually notice when the managers left.

What I did hear was a swallow and saw Paul setting down his wineglass.

My eyes widened. "You drank the wine? I told you not to drink the wine."

"You were serious?"

"Of course I was serious." I looked around the table. "When am I not serious?"

"A lot of the time," Paul said. Then added, "I hope."

At his last comment, Juniper tried to hide her giggle with a cough.

"Holt, what's the matter?" Britt asked, sounding full paramedic.

"It's just, if anything here were to be poisoned, the wine's a good place to hide it."

Paul's hand went to his chest, and he cleared his throat.

Sienna was immediately by his side. "How do you feel?"

"I...I don't know." Paul shook his head. "It could all be in my head, but on the other hand..." When he trailed off, everyone looked at me like I had the answers.

"I mean"—I ran a hand through my hair—"it might not be poisoned."

"Okay." Brittany had heard enough. "We're going to the hospital just to be safe. Sienna, are you good to drive?"

"Yes. We're parked in the other lot," she said. "Let me run and get the car. I'll be right back."

"All right, Paul," Brittany said. "Let's get you outside." Britt was totally calm. What kind of things had she gone through to stay so coolheaded?

Paul gave a forced laugh. "No need to be so serious. I'm probably fine."

"Sure," Brittany said. "Now, come on."

Britt and I walked on either side of Paul, who did a remarkable job of not looking scared. As we waited on the front steps for Sienna, Brittany rested her hand on my arm. "I think you should stay here. This could be a long night."

I was opening my mouth to say *What are boyfriends for?* when Britt added, "If we need anything from the house, you'll be able to bring it."

"Um," is what I ended up saying, and before I knew it Brittany was pressing a kiss to my cheek and running with Paul to Sienna's car. They sped up the driveway, Sienna driving straight into the sunset. Leaning against the railing, I let out a sigh, hoping I was just being paranoid.

I didn't want to go back to the dining room, and there was no way I was eating the food. Still, I couldn't leave Juniper totally abandoned.

But when I returned, our table was empty. Juniper was gone. Instead, there was a table with plates full of food and filled wineglasses. It was sort of spooky.

I made my way upstairs, since Juniper must've gone up to our rooms.

But Juniper wasn't on the sectional or in either bathroom, and the light was off in the girls' room. "Juniper?" I called.

No answer. Maybe she'd taken Chouzie on a walk?

Then I heard it. Heavy breathing. Leaving the front door wide open—so someone could hear my screams—I crept toward the sound. It was coming from the girls' bedroom. Their door was half-closed and the light was off. The breathing grew louder as I approached. I pictured a faceless goon lurking in the shadows.

Could whoever it was have Juniper? Or were they waiting for me?

After a moment of indecision, I shoved the door open and turned the lights on. Chouzie gave a surprised dog snort and stood up from his dog bed.

Chouzie. The heavy breathing was Chouzie? I was sweating through my shirt because of a chow chow?

He gave a low growl of displeasure for being disturbed, then lay back down, and the heavy breathing resumed.

Sagging against the doorframe, I began massaging my temples. Juniper had given me this headache. She was the one who'd suggested confronting Quirky Sue and trying to get a murder confession.

Wait.

I straightened.

She wouldn't.

What was I thinking? Of course she had.

I was running downstairs a moment later. Because Juniper would absolutely take the opportunity of being separated from the group to question Sue.

Maybe I was paranoid assuming Paul had been poisoned and maybe Juniper wasn't in mortal danger, but I wasn't taking any chances. I rushed past the guests in the dining room and charged into the kitchen. Brad and Hannah jumped at my entrance.

"How can I help you?" Brad asked as Hannah said, "You're not allowed back here."

"Juniper. Where's Juniper?" I wheezed before collapsing onto the floor. Dark spots crowded my vision, and I was on my hands and knees, trying to get enough air. Turns out running was a bad idea given the state of my lungs.

"Here, sit back. Take some deep breaths," Brad said from beside me.

I clawed wildly at his shirt. "Juniper?" I repeated. "Or Sue? Have you seen either of them?"

Neither one answered. Instead, a paper bag was shoved at my face. "Breathe."

I rolled my eyes. We were getting nowhere. They wouldn't help me until my breathing had regulated, so I started breathing into the bag.

Honestly, some people can be so finicky. I'd had a little accident, and my lungs were recovering. Just because I collapsed on their kitchen floor was no reason for them to panic.

"Should we call an ambulance?" Hot Hannah asked, standing behind her husband.

I shook my head. "Don't bother. I'm great." Then I thought of Juniper and grabbed my phone. My sister had programmed Cop Kid's info into my phone, and it felt like an appropriate time to give the man a call—or after I'd taken a few more breaths from the paper bag.

Pulling up my contacts, I realized I had a problem. I didn't actually know Cop Kid's name. Scrolling through contacts wouldn't help. It's not like I remember all the names in my phone...so many people from random work retreats.

"What's the area code?" I asked.

"Uh, 509," Brad said, glancing from me to Hannah.

If I kept acting like this, he'd be signaling her to call 911.

Didn't matter.

When I typed *509* into the search bar, a *Detective Hagen* jumped out from the results. Worked for me. Pressing the call button, I began second-guessing whether it was the right person as soon as the ringing began.

"Detective Hagen," a laid-back voice said. It was definitely Cop Kid.

"This is Holt. Holt Jacobs," I said.

"Been a while," he said. "What do you need?"

"Can you come by Rose's Vineyard? It's probably nothing. I'm probably making stuff up, but..." I had to take a deep breath—somehow there wasn't enough air in the kitchen. "I'd feel better if you stopped by."

Muffled sounds of a car door slamming and an engine turning on came through the line. "I'm on my way," Cop Kid said.

"Thanks," I said.

"Oh, and, Holt?"

"Yeah?"

"Sit tight, okay? I'll be right over."

Brad and Hannah were watching me, their expressions unreadable. Suddenly I wasn't so sure Sue was the killer. Maybe it was Hannah and Brad.

"I have to go," I said and ended the call.

I lumbered to my feet and began backing toward the dining room. "Well, it's been great. Thanks for the hospitality and the paper bag." I was still holding the bag and shoved it unceremoniously into my pocket.

"Anyway," I said, "I gotta run."

"Hold on," Brad said, taking a step toward me.

I panicked and fled.

Maybe Brad and Hannah hadn't been about to kidnap me, but I wasn't taking any chances.

CHAPTER 13

The light was fading into dusk as I escaped outside. I'd forgotten the easiest way to find Juniper. Why had I called the police before I called her? That was pretty stupid.

Moving away from Rose's Repose, I tried calling, and all I got was ringing before I was sent to Juniper's voicemail. I hung up and texted: *Where are you?*

Without consciously deciding to, I'd been walking the path to the winery. Up ahead there was a flicker of movement and the slam of a door.

Brad and Hannah were back at the house. It had to be Sue or Juniper. I sped up my walk while moving slowly enough that I wouldn't need to start gasping into a paper bag again.

I eased the side door open, finding the winery blanketed in darkness. I swallowed. Could Juniper really be in here? Closing the door silently behind me, I began creeping down the deserted rows.

The final rays of light filtered through the windows. But it was mostly dark. Anyone could've hidden in the shadows of the massive wine vats.

I checked my phone. Juniper hadn't replied to my text. Hopefully, she wasn't being held hostage farther inside the winery. Still, as a precaution I turned my phone to silent, not wanting an unexpected text to give away my location.

Faint scuffling echoed through the space. Was that from another human, or were rats patrolling the building? Was it bad that sharing the space with a murderer scared me less than a family of rats?

Coming to the end of a row of tanks, I saw a light shining from under the door that stored the bottled wine. Moving carefully to the door, I listened. If Juniper was in there, I should be able to hear her talking.

Someone was in there moving things around. But there were no voices. Quirky Sue had to be inside. The question was, did she have Juniper with her? Maybe Sue had gagged my sister to keep her from talking.

There was muttering, but I couldn't make out any words. And I couldn't tell whether Sue was talking to herself or to Juniper.

Should I barge in?

Cop Kid was on his way.

Should I wait?

I was standing in front of the storage room door when it opened, and I was eye to eye with Average Joe.

He gasped and stumbled backward, dropping an open bottle of wine. The glass shattered, spilling its red contents across the floor. Beyond him a table had been set up like a mad scientist's lair, with glass tubes and beakers holding different amounts of pinkish liquid.

"You shouldn't be here," Joe said.

I found my jaw was hanging open at my peek into Frankenstein's lab. "Um, yeah. Sorry. I was looking for my sister."

Joe crossed his arms. "She isn't here."

"Right." I gave a hollow laugh. "You're absolutely right."

Average Joe was dressed in work clothes identical to what he'd worn the past two days. He'd just left the hospital. Didn't he have sweats?

He was watching me too intensely.

I couldn't turn my back on him—which I'd have to do to leave. So I did what many desperate men have tried before. I attempted small talk.

"Impressive you're already back to work in the winery. After yesterday's wine bath, I've been doing my best to steer clear of the smell."

Small talk is dumb. I know it's dumb. But Joe didn't respond at all. The guy I'd rescued at great personal risk, who'd later accused me of pushing him, had nothing to say. Not a *sorry* or a *thank you*.

Joe stood there, his back framed by the storage room's light, his body slightly hunched. If it came to a footrace, his lungs had to be in worse shape than mine. Since he'd been in the wine longer, I should be able to outrun him before we both collapsed. Still, he had home-field advantage.

I really didn't want to run. But alone in an empty winery, Average Joe was creeping me out.

"Um, that's quite the setup you've got there," I tried, pointing to his worktable.

"It's for the rosé." Joe gazed almost lovingly at the table. "The wine's simple enough to make, but when Rose got her hands on it, it was magic. I've been trying to discover her secret." He looked at me almost shyly. "It might not make sense to you, but the rosé tasted like Rose."

He was right. It didn't make sense. But he was a scary guy in an abandoned building, so I nodded understandingly.

"Brad promised to find the best vintner to help re-create the process. I thought she'd come the other day, but..." As Joe trailed off, the color drained from his face. Almost like he felt guilty.

Guilty?

Wait. Had he killed Tasha?

Whoever had stabbed Tasha would've gotten blood on their clothes. Quirky Sue had been wearing a pastel dress. If it'd been her, someone would have seen the stains, and there was no way she could have changed outfits without being noticed. But Average Joe? His wardrobe was nothing but black T-shirts and dark pants. He could have easily changed and no one would have known.

Everything I thought I had known shifted. If Joe had just played it cool, I wouldn't have put two and two together. But somehow he'd mistaken Tasha for the vintner.

"You were behind the bar with Sue," I said. "You took the Venetian corkscrew."

I'd rescued a murderer.

There was still the little question of who'd pushed him into the vat, but since Joe made a menacing growl and switched off the storeroom lights, I'd have to figure out that detail a little later.

"You shouldn't be here," Joe said again.

I didn't know what Joe's plan was, but I thought it best to hide. My eyes hadn't fully adjusted to the dark, but I tried to lose myself in the rows of wine containers.

My heart was pounding in my ears. I needed to get to an exit. But which one? And where was I? In the game of cat and mouse, Joe had the advantage.

"Rose had to do it. Had to find one last way to punish me." Joe's voice echoed against the metal containers, and I couldn't tell where it came from. "She stole my life!" Then he muttered something unintelligible, before saying, "I lost my fiancée, and Rose gave the winery to a stranger, but she couldn't stop. She had to take the rosé."

"So you killed your daughter?" The words came out thoughtlessly. Joe really didn't need help finding my position. And Tasha being Joe's daughter was an educated guess.

"That wasn't my daughter!" The voice was louder and angrier. "The adoption was closed. Rose said there was no way of tracking her down."

We'd been right? Joe was the father of Rose's baby?

In the quiet, I heard Joe's footsteps, seeming to come at me from every direction. I had to pick an exit and hope he wasn't there waiting. I slid along the shadows, barely daring to breathe.

"You've been talking to Hannah!" Joe's voice had come from the opposite side of my container, and I swallowed a gasp. "Believing Rose had left the winery to our kid made Hannah and Sue feel better. But Rose couldn't know. She chose a random woman who was the right age, just to mess with me one last time." His voice grew distant as he moved farther away.

All those group pictures played through my mind. Why had Rose caught my attention when I had no clue who she was? Was it subconscious recognition? Could I have recognized Tasha's mother when I hadn't recognized Tasha?

So I didn't know for sure, but it wasn't like Joe could get a paternity test in the next five minutes. I took a risk. "I knew Tasha. She looked like Rose. Natasha was your daughter."

A green exit sign glowed a few yards away. All I'd need to do was sprint from the last vat to the door. Suddenly the overhead lights came on, and Average Joe was right in front of me.

His face was ghastly. "But that would mean..."

"Rose lied about the closed adoption. She knew Tasha was her daughter."

"No, no." Joe took a step toward me. "That woman was supposed to be a vintner. She was supposed to help me. But instead she was a spy who thought she could lie, and trick, and use me just like Rose had. It's bad enough Rose gave away my home to a stranger, but when I found out Natasha was spying on my work, I just got so mad, I..." Joe hung his head.

"Tasha wasn't spying," I said, watching him carefully. I was prepared for Joe to lunge at me, but so far he only stood there—blocking the exit. "She didn't know you thought she was a vintner. All Tasha was doing was looking at the property her Mom had left her."

Joe groaned and sort of crumpled to the floor. "I can't believe this. I never meant to kill her." He buried his head in his hands. "But I was holding the corkscrew and showing her the rosé, thinking she was the vintner. Then, when she said she'd inherited the winery..." Joe looked up at me helplessly. "I don't know what happened."

Joe was between me and the exit, and I was crashing post–adrenaline rush. In theory I could have walked around him, but to my horror, I found my legs buckling, and then I was sitting on the floor just like Joe.

I don't recommend carbon dioxide poisoning. That stuff lingers.

Average Joe took my sitting as some sort of invitation to open up. "I was engaged to a model when it happened. Rose made a pass at me and..." He shook his head. "I messed everything up. I tried to fix things with my fiancée, but she didn't want anything more to do with me. Then I tried to make a family with Rose, but"—Joe gave a twisted smile—"she never gave me another chance."

I squeezed my eyes shut. How had Rose so manipulated the world around her? And she'd never even be punished for driving Joe crazy.

"I'm sorry," I said. Though I really shouldn't be apologizing to the guy who'd killed my ex-girlfriend. How messed up was it I felt bad for the guy?

"Thanks." Joe's voice was subdued.

"How did you end up in the wine vat?" I asked.

Joe winced. "Sue confronted me about the missing corkscrew." He rubbed the back of his head. "When I confessed, she hit me over the head with a bottle and pushed me in."

Sue had confronted him? So she'd figured out he'd taken the corkscrew.

Hold on. That morning walk she'd taken through the vineyard...She hadn't been *getting some air* or *grieving the loss of Rose*. She'd been looking for Average Joe. When Quirky Sue didn't find him in the vineyard, she'd confronted him in the winery.

But that meant...Quirky Sue had managed to lie to Juniper? Fascinating. I'd underestimated her.

"So"—I scrubbed a hand over my face, feeling less bad for the guy—"you blamed me. You said I pushed you, because if they arrested Sue, she'd tell the police you'd killed Tasha?"

Joe's head rolled back, and he stared at the rafters. "Not one of my finest moments. Then I felt extra bad when I found out you were the one who rescued me. Thanks, by the way."

"Anytime," I muttered, though we both knew that was a lie. "And why didn't Sue turn you in?"

Joe almost laughed. "We talked about that on the ride from the hospital. Sue didn't want to be arrested for attempted murder, so we called it even. I wouldn't squeal if she wouldn't."

I must have heard him wrong.

"You got in a car with her? The woman who tried to kill you?"

"I was trying to get away with murder." He shrugged. "You'd be surprised what you'll find yourself doing."

I gave a half nod. *Speak for yourself, buddy.*

"What was my daughter like?" Joe asked, his voice subdued.

What could I tell him about Tasha, the cool girlfriend I'd had in college?

"Well, she was getting a psych degree..." *She dumped me.* "Uh, she was...right-handed."

"Really?" Joe's head fell into his hands. "I'm right-handed."

Yeah. Most people are.

Joe sniffed and wiped his eyes. "It's over, then." Suddenly, he started laughing hysterically. "Are you happy, Rose?" he yelled at the rafters. "Is this what you wanted?"

It was definitely time to go. Slowly rising to my feet, I offered Joe a hand up. "I called the detective. It'll be better if you turn yourself in."

Joe held my hand a second longer and gave it a little shake. "Thank you," he said.

We walked out of the winery and into quite a mess.

CHAPTER 14

I t was like I'd walked into a hostage situation. There were a lot more police than just Cop Kid. Floodlights were on, and people were shouting.

"Raise your hands," Joe said from beside me.

Right. They were all here for us. Fantastic.

My hands went up, and then Joe and I were both directed to kneel. I almost got a face full of ground, when I tripped getting to my knees.

It didn't take long before Cop Kid was beside me, helping me up. He tried to look stern. "You're a real pain."

I shrugged. "One of my best features."

"Did Joe hurt you?"

"What?" I looked to Joe, who was still kneeling but with the addition of handcuffs. "No. He was turning himself in."

"I see," the cop said. He led me past the first responders. "Good instincts calling me. Now, if you'd just stayed put when I told you to, it'd be a perfect night."

"Hey." I raised my hands. "I thought Juniper was in trouble."

Cop Kid's eyes widened. "Oh, she is."

Before I could ask what he meant, Juniper yelled, "Holt!" and vaulted herself into my arms.

Good thing Cop Kid was there; he kept both of us upright.

"We'll talk later," he said.

Juniper had made it inside the police perimeter and began asking what happened, then if I was all right, never giving me a chance to answer. During her barrage of questions, she led me to where Brittany, Paul, and Sienna were waiting on the other side of the barricade.

Britt's shoulders relaxed the moment our eyes met. "You look awful," she said, brushing hair off my forehead.

I tried to frown, but it was so good to see her. "Hello, to you, too," I said, wrapping my arms around her and holding on tightly.

"Glad you're all right," Paul said, giving my back a pat and effectively ruining my moment with his sister.

"Thanks. Same to you," I said.

When I stepped out of our hug, Sienna was there, waiting on tiptoes to press a kiss to my cheek. "You had us worried," she said.

"Sorry about that." I held Sienna's gaze until she seemed satisfied with my well-being. Then I wrapped an arm around Britt's back, still needing to hold her close. Since everyone was watching me like I might be in shock, I asked, "Was the wine poisoned?"

"No, it was not," Brittany said as we slowly made our way from the winery and to seats on the lighted patio.

"Oh." I ran a hand through my hair. "My bad."

Paul shrugged. "Juniper let us know there wasn't any poison before we got to the hospital, so we just turned around."

My voice hardened. "And how did Juniper know this?"

And just like that, no one would look at me.

"You have to understand," Juniper said, turning on the doe eyes. "We were all worried about Paul, and if he'd been poisoned, it would have been good to know what it was..."

"Juniper," I growled, "get to the point."

"So, I kind of talked to Sue."

I rubbed a hand across my face, not at all surprised. "Of course you did." I left my chair and began pacing. "Do you know how scared I was when I couldn't find you? I thought you'd confronted a killer."

Juniper giggled nervously. "Turns out I was confronting an attempted killer, while you were talking to the real killer."

"That's because I was looking for you!" I sank back into my chair, so worn out. "I wasn't trying to talk to the real killer."

"Sue was right," Juniper said, laughing nervously. "You are heroic."

I cleared my throat. "If you're trying to win me over with compliments, you'll need to keep going."

Juniper tossed back her hair. "Nope. That's all you're getting."

When I raised an eyebrow, Juniper stuck her tongue out.

Real mature.

Brittany stood by my chair and rested her hands on my shoulders. "What exactly happened in there?"

"Oh, you know," I said, resting my head against her arm. "He accidentally confessed, then tried to trap me when I ran. We ended up talking about Tasha, and I got him to turn himself in to the cops."

"Ohhh." Juniper jumped up and down on her feet. "You got someone to confess and turn themselves in? I'm a good influence."

My head snapped up. "Good influence? No. Absolutely not."

Juniper's voice turned cartoonish. *"And he would have gotten away with it, if not for us meddling kids."*

"Juniper!" Brittany said.

I smirked at Juniper's shocked expression. "I'm a good influence for Brittany." That was when my girlfriend swatted the back of my head.

"Anyway," Juniper said, "before Detective Hagen showed up and arrested her, Sue told me everything. All about how—"

"—she figured out Joe killed Tasha?" I interrupted.

Juniper faltered. "Yes, but also how she—"

"—confronted and then attacked him?"

Brittany gave a soft laugh, while Juniper wrinkled her nose, at a loss for words. Then her eyes brightened. "But she couldn't tell the police Joe was the killer because—"

I did my best to impersonate Sue, holding my hands up in innocence. "—*if I gave Joe up, I'd have to confess to attempted murder.*"

Paul surprised us all by saying, "Holt really is a good influence."

Juniper's eyes almost bugged out of her head, and I'm pretty sure she had to bite her tongue to stop from sticking it out at Paul.

Paul chuckled. Not at all bothered by Juniper's annoyance. "Let's go get burgers," he said. "I'm starving."

We had skipped supper.

"We're in," Brittany said, knowing without asking I was ready for food.

Paul tossed his keys in the air and caught them easily. "I'll drive."

Paul and Sienna headed for his car, with Juniper trailing a few feet behind them, still puzzled by the turn of events.

Britt offered me a hand up. "Shall we?" she asked.

I grinned as I held her hand. "We shall."

"You may have been worried about your sister," Britt said quietly. "But I was pretty worried when you wouldn't answer the phone."

"You called?" I tried to sound casual, but my shoulders were expanding, and there was no hiding how happy that made me.

Brittany bumped into me as we walked. "Of course I called. I called as soon as Juniper let me know Paul wasn't poisoned. Then, when you didn't answer, I started texting."

We were close to the car and the others had already loaded in, but I stopped and checked my phone.

Britt: *Call me back.*

Britt: *Where are you?*

Britt: *Holt.*

Britt: *Paul's fine. Are you?*

Britt: *We're almost at the vineyard. Where are you?*

Britt: *I'm worried.*

Britt: *Please answer.*

I lifted an eyebrow. "You texted seven times?"

Britt tucked invisible strands of hair behind her ears. "Well..."

I did a goofy dance around Britt. "You were positively spamming me."

She tried to be serious, but her eyes were sparkling. "Don't let it go to your head."

I smirked. "I wouldn't dream of it. Now give me a sec so I can take a screenshot and make this my phone's wallpaper."

Just then my screen changed to show an incoming call from Mom. Either Mom was calling because she'd sensed I'd been in danger, or she wanted me to RSVP for Christmas.

"Holt?" Brittany asked.

Britt's brown eyes were looking up at me, and something around my heart tightened. I knew what I had to do. Without freezing, over-thinking, or chickening out, I asked, "Would you like to join my whole family for Christmas?"

"Sure," Britt said without a moment's hesitation.

"What?" I took a step back. "Just like that? Are you sure? It'll be my whole family under one roof. With Casey's kids and Juniper's dog, it'll be super loud." I shuddered. "Moms, and dogs, and kids."

Britt took a step closer. "Do you want me there?"

"Yeah?" I tugged at my hair. "But, like, you didn't even think about it. Like, what will your family do without you?"

Brittany tilted her head toward Juniper sitting in the car. "I may have had some time to think about it."

I stiffened, and Britt put a hand on my chest.

"With your parents living in Australia, this seemed like the best option. And"—a shy smile tugged at her lips—"I'd like the chance to get to know them. All the moms, and dogs, and kids."

"You're sure?"

"Absolutely."

I'd missed the first call from Mom, but then the screen lit up with her name again. When I answered, I didn't bother with a greeting. "I'll be there for Christmas, and I'm bringing Britt." Then I hung up without waiting for an answer.

For a moment I glanced at the car. I wanted to get revenge on Juniper for blabbing, but I wanted to kiss Britt more.

Wrapping my arms around Brittany, I grinned as I lowered my lips to hers. Right before we kissed, I whispered, "You have no idea what you're in for."

What do ax murderers, stolen stockings, and a house full of relatives have in common? Read Holt's next mystery *A Not So Cozy Christmas* to find out.

Ready for a Holt Jacobs snack-sized mystery? Sign up for my newsletter at *lilystirling.com* and receive a copy of *Holt Jacobs & The Mystery Of The Missing Sunglasses*, plus delightful every-other-week emails.

Bravo!

Way to read a book!

You're so smart.

A Not So Rosy Vintage is probably my favorite Holt Jacobs book. I love the mirrored friend groups between this story's main characters and suspects. It's like the best (and worst) parts of summer camp.

Another reason I really like this book is that it shows more of Holt's relationship with Juniper—the good, the bad, and the hilarious...Imagine what it was like when they were kids living under one roof!

What did you love about *A Not So Rosy Vintage*? If you have the time, let me and potential readers know by leaving a review.

Ready for a story full of *moms, and dogs, and kids*? Then get ready for Holt's next mystery, *A Not So Cozy Christmas*.

An ax murderer over the holidays is the perfect challenge for any sarcastic sleuth, and Holt Jacobs is up for the challenge!

If you want to hang out, join my newsletter at *lilystirling.com*. You'll get every-other-week updates, plus Holt's snack-sized story, *Holt Jacobs & The Mystery Of The Missing Sunglasses*.

Thanks for reading!

~ *Lily Stirling*

ABOUT THE AUTHOR

Lily Stirling is the writer of the Holt Jacobs Mystery series.

She has spent a quarter of a century living in the Pacific Northwest. Lily was born in Idaho, but her family moved to Washington around the time she could read chapter books.

Mysteries have always delighted her, from listening to The Hardy Boys on car trips to watching episodes of Psych.

As for sarcastic families, when she's not writing about one, she's living in one.

ACKNOWLEDGEMENTS

I'm so thankful for everyone on my production team. You make my book sparkle!

Production Team:

Developmental Editor ~ Kristen Weber

Copyeditor ~ Penina Lopez

Proofreader ~ Elaini Caruso

Cover Designer ~ Mariah Sinclair

———◆◇◆———

A huge thanks goes to my parents for their constant love and support. You make parenting look easy.

Thanks to Alessandra, Terezia, Ava, and everyone at Inkers Mastermind. It's been incredible to have such a supportive writing community.

Finally, thank *you* for reading my book and all the back matter. I hope you love Holt's winery adventure as much as I do!

Until next time!

Lily Stirling

HOLT JACOBS MYSTERY SERIES

A Not So Shocking Murder
A Not So Rustic Retreat
A Not So Rosy Vintage
A Not So Cozy Christmas

www.ingramcontent.com/pod-product-compliance
Lightning Source LLC
Chambersburg PA
CBHW032010170626
46807CB00006B/2735